5 r

Stories, Fables & Other Diversions

Stories
Fables
&
Other
Diversions

BY HOWARD NEMEROV

 Godine · Boston · MCMLXXI

ACKNOWLEDGMENTS

"The Outage," first published in *Perspective.*

"The Executive," first published in *Esquire.*

"Mudras of Meetings," first published in *The Bennington College Review.*

"Unbelievable Characters," first published in *Esquire.*

"The Escapist," first published in *The Virginia Quarterly Review.*

"The Native in the World," first published in *The Harvard Advocate.*

"The Idea of a University," first published in *The Reporter.*

"The Nature of the Task," first published in *The Virginia Quarterly Review.*

"Digressions Around a Crow," first published by *Carleton Miscellany.*
Copyright, Carleton College.

Table of Contents

The Twelve and the One

IT IS A HARD flight from Trent to Rome, one has the Apennines to get over, but all the same a party of twelve Jews made the journey one Halloween, riding a rushing wind beneath the brilliant moon in a straggling V formation. A thirteenth voyager of the air had seemed to be of the party at its setting forth, but he flew feebly and was soon distanced.

Beginning the descent to Rome, the twelve made out without difficulty the dome of St. Peter's. Their leader took them in a steep gliding turn—their beards swept askew, their eyes glowing like coals fanned by the wind—once round the dome and down, down past the walls of the Vatican and presently through a window. Like great bats the twelve Jews fluttered heavily down long corridors, through sequences of empty chambers, until presently they reached the room where the Holy Father slept. There they let down their feet and alighted and stood.

They said nothing, yet the Holy Father awakened almost at once. Raising himself up on one elbow he made out, blinking, the twelve by the gloomy illumination of a small night-light on his bedside table.

"I have expected you," said His Holiness. "I have awaited your coming in fear and sorrow, you Jews of Trent."

The twelve Jews said nothing, they looked at the man in the bed who looked at them, and in their look the man could read, so empty as it was, whatever his soul required him to read; for in themselves the twelve faces were as expressionless as the face of the small electric clock on the table beside him, whose golden second hand spun silently around.

"You had the right to come," His Holiness went on. "Of the countless millions of the dead of all the ages that tonight would seek the living, and of the millions of the faithful dead that tonight might seek especially Ourself, I knew, I anticipated in fear all day, O Jews of Trent, that you would have the highest claim.

"O, it was a terrible thing we did to you," he cried out suddenly; and then, in a lower voice, "so long ago, so long ago. But not the near five hundred years from then to this, not all the moments of those centuries with all their sufferings of all their peoples between birth and death, can remedy your sufferings or my grief."

The twelve Jews appeared to listen attentively, but said nothing. It was this neutral or even polite silence that the Holy Father began helplessly filling up with words—as though all the words ever spoken could fill up a silence!

"What can man do? what can he do?" he cried, raising himself in the bed and stretching out his arms appealing. "I see the accusation glaring from your eyes, I grant its justice, take upon myself its truth, that all those centuries ago the Church, afflicted by the superstitious ignorance of those times, did hold you accountable for the ritual murder of an infant boy named Simon. You were tortured to make you confess; some of you died under the torture; none of you confessed. The rest we executed. How can you forgive us? How can you forgive me?"

The silence which had been hiding underneath his words appeared again as soon as he paused for breath; and the Jews did nothing to break it, but stood as patiently as before. More persuasively, more pleadingly now, the Holy Father went on.

"As the spiritual head of Catholic Christendom," he said, "I have acknowledged my sorrow, your injustice, our most grievous fault. For if the Church is one, and it is, if its spiritual succession proceeds unbroken from Peter, and it does, then am I responsible to the height and heaviness of my office for much vileness in the world, much obscenity, much horror—and much absurdity, too.

"And yet I plead with you, you Jews of Trent, for this night gifted with the privilege of the air, that I of all men am your friend, that I of all men made what poor and plentifully foolish reparation the nature of this vale of tears affords. Scholars I sent, learned divines I sent, gifted in historical studies, to look back deeply into time, to see that injustice without remedy had been done—and I did not flinch from crying out before the world that all was not as it had seemed in your time, and that the Holy Roman Catholic Church would bow itself in sorrow to say that it had grievously offended and to ask forgiveness of the Lord. Jews of Trent, no man can return to the time that was, no man is able to rescind your sufferings or dry the tears of your agony. But I plead with you all to say now whether I have not done all that is possible for man to do. I have proclaimed your innocence and our offence, and even in the face of the not unreasonable jeering of cynic and skeptic set an example to the world that the Church is able to acknowledge its former errors, and repent, and reform."

The Holy Father's eloquence left the silence as it had been, nor did the golden second hand of the bedside clock cease from revolving as he spoke.

"I have said," he now resumed, "all that I could have said. And you say nothing, Jews of Trent. Have you no charity? Can it be still that you are as you were, a stubborn and a stiff-necked people? Are you vengeful? against Ourself, that meant you only good? I need not have done all that I did, I need not have opened the graves and let you out to stand before me as my judges with your silence, with the fiery empty darkness of your terrible eyes, I might have let the dead bury their dead and none the wiser. There's much injustice done in the world. I could have passed by on the other side and affected not to see. You could not then have troubled me. Ah, would that I had!" And the old man sank back among the pillows as though in full admission of his helplessness.

"Would that you had indeed, Holy Father!" broke in a thin and shrilling voice from the window, where alighted now the thirteenth voyager from Trent. "For I am Simon the child, and the wrong you sought to right did me a grievous wrong in turn. Because of my ritual murder at the hands of the Jews of Trent I was exalted mightily to be a martyr and to be a witness to the truth of the sufferings of another Child. And, infant as I was, I reached so high as to the rank of Blessed, that in the region around Trent the Mass might be said in my name, people might venerate the bones I left behind, or my little few playthings, and, my story being told over, I was remembered among the living. Now all that in a stroke you and your Sacred Congregation of Rites have mercilessly taken from me. I was an infant child, without speech or understanding. But I *was* murdered, and it gave me a distinction, I tell you, there—there, you understand," and suddenly his voice faded into an almost indistinct murmur, "there, among the others, afterwards . . . "

It had been the Holy Father's turn to be silent during this outburst, and now he looked long and wonderingly at the child.

"Dear Child," he said slowly, and in a voice broken with sighs that presently were sobs, "I sorrow for thine innocence, hurt regardless and without intention in the various woundings of the world. Would that I might restore to thee thy honors among men. But it is beyond my power as a man. O, I see thee," he cried out, raising himself again, "I see thee all thirteen, and my mind is carried back to visions of the Child Himself and of the Twelve that left the world to follow Him, and I think I see the chapters of the sacred story once again unfold from the crib in wintry Bethlehem to the Cross on Calvary at the first of Spring, and I, an old man, tired, near to death himself, think of the manifold ills of this the world, and ask thee, thee the Child and thee the elders twelve, I ask thee as I ask my God, cannot you now forgive one another?"

Now all the thirteen, still in silence, withdrew their eyes from the Pope of Rome, and the twelve looked at the one, while the one looked at the twelve. The hour of three struck on the great bells above, unnoticed by the little golden second hand that never faltered on its rounds.

And it seemed now that some among the Jews made to stoop to the little boy, perhaps to comfort, perhaps to caress, to say some soothing, helpless, tender thing, perhaps even to lift him up upon their grown-ups' shoulders and take turns, seeing he was so small and weak, to carry him pickaback across the snowy mountains to their home in Trent. If spirits had shoulders, so it might have been. But as it was, and now the twelve Jews one by one lifted themselves heavily and hoveringly into air and left by way of the window, as it was, poor Simon had to limp back to Trent on (as they used to say) a wing and a prayer, according to the impenetrable secret will of God who made the heavens and the earth and the suffering. And the Holy Father slept.

The Outage

IN FAMILIES that cared for customary ways the telling of the story was assigned to the oldest man present—grandpa it might be, or great-uncle—with only his wife allowed to correct him or bring him back if he strayed; his wife, or else, if he were widowed, one of the other old women. He would begin after the traditional holiday dinner, at the time of drawing of curtains and lighting of lamps, with the families arrayed around him. The middle generation, the fathers and mothers and uncles and aunts, some of whom could remember and some of whom only thought they remembered, were expected to contribute to the recital only their choral assent at the high moments; while the children—well, the children had to ask questions, and on this occasion their questions would be received with good humor, though not invariably answered. In return, they shared in the convention by pretending to be hearing the story for the first time, though only the youngest of them really were.

The grandfather began.

"Once long ago," he said, "there was electricity. It was not a thing, such as table or chair, but a force, a very great force; it was not a thing, but it did many things. One of the things it did was fill houses with light. We used to be able to press that little black doohickey on the wall there, and this room would become bright enough to read in right away; the light would come from those pear-shaped glass things called bulbs that you see hung from the ceiling; or sometimes from long glass tubes that would flicker prettily at first before they settled to a steady shine.

"That wasn't all electricity could do—there were a great many more things than that—but it was the most wonderful and the one we most took for granted. Whenever you walked into a room that was darker than you wanted it to be, you would press one of those things set into the wall—right by the door, for convenience—and the room would immediately light up, spread with an even, unwavering light.

"One thing the electricity did, it made the world of those days practically free of demons and ghosts. They always existed, of course, but by turning on the lights you automatically made them leave the house; so that for all practical purposes it was as if there weren't any."

The children began looking at one another a little doubtfully in the firelight, the lamplight, and from the shadows a-round the grown-ups' knees. It was a nice idea for a story, their glances seemed to say, but how seriously ought it to be taken?

"With this electricity," the grandfather went on, "you could also run a great many different machines. You know what machines are, you see them every day on your way to school, standing out in the weather with a kind of hulking patience—cars, trucks, and so on; in some spots you can see the fine colors they had before they rusted so. Those particular machines didn't quite *run* by electricity, but they had to be started by electricity. . . . I like to think that if electric power came back they would some of them be right and ready to go, just like that. It used to be such a fine thing to see, on the big roads, the lanes of traffic streaming away in both directions as far as the eye could see, and all the colors of the speeding cars that flashed in the sunlight . . . or else at night the headlight beams driving their moving cones of light into and through the shadows . . . "

"Tell them more about in the house," his wife reminded him. She thought perhaps he was becoming too rhapsodic.

"In the house?" the old man said, "Well, in the house I used to lie awake some nights counting up the number of items we owned that ran by electricity. The power came in the house from those rubbery-looking ropes and cords and cables you still see carried on poles along the street, and once it got into the house this power was good for almost anything: it cooked, it ironed, it washed, it kept people warm and kept their food cold; if you had the right machines it would even sharpen pencils, or tell time, or make ice cubes—it would freeze the water into miniature blocks—or run typewriters, or do the sewing . . . "

There is some trouble in narrating things you have experienced to people who have never known their like at all: you never know when you are leaving out some essential point, and you never know what strange shape your understanding takes inside another mind. The children were attentively trying to imagine a sort of stuff that oozed or crept along or through those rubbery-looking ropes and came into your house and went right to the ironing-board and *did the ironing*. But the only way they had of doing this was to imagine mother standing there with the iron in hand, and then subtract from that picture mother, iron—maybe ironing-board as well?—which left the clothes and—and what?

But the old man had his story to tell, it was all present to his memory, and he went right on, getting vaguer as he went, about all the marvelous things that could be done by electricity—only by this time he had for the most part dropped that word and was speaking instead of *power*, and *the power*. Also it was observable, though not by the children, that he was moving ever further from his own experienced knowledge, and talking instead of such things as mains and generators and transformers and dynamoes; of hydraulic stations and even of what he called The Central Power Station and the Hydroelectric Grid, which last seemed to be like a gigantic invisible spider's web—without a spider—that began in one place and went all over the world.

"Now that's enough, Arthur," the old woman put in after

a while of this sort of thing. "It's only confusing the children, and you're not getting on with the story."

"I just wanted to give the whole picture," said the grandfather. "I wanted the children to see it as it was. But all right, all right."

"The story," he began anew, "is simply told, for its climax is not, as in an ordinary story, the happening of something, but, instead, the happening of nothing. We had all these things I've been telling you of, and then, instantly, on this very day, and almost at this time of day, in fact—there it all wasn't. It was gone. Just as the wives were beginning to cook the supper, as the men were coming home from work and looking forward to the evening news on the TV—you never even let me tell them about television," he said complainingly, "but that glass-fronted chest over there in the corner, with the plants on top—you children may not believe this, but it used to light up and pictures would come out on the glass part, moving pictures. People would be there dancing and singing and telling you what was happening everywhere . . . "

"You mean there used to be people in that box?" a child asked, and another child snickered, but softly, imagining how tiny those people would have had to be.

"No, not exactly *in* the box," grandfather said, and stopped. But an uncle permissibly intervened to save the situation by saying rather impressively, "It was done by what they used to call a *cathode ray tube*." Several people murmured "*cathode ray tube*" in a ragged chorus, and renewed silence seemed to show that this explanation satisfied.

"Now what you want to imagine if you can," the grandfather resumed, "is the bewilderment and the helplessness. What's most important to see is that none of us so much as knew what had happened. We assumed, of course, that it was an ordinary power failure and would be put right in a matter of minutes or at most a few hours. There even used to be a joke about such things, which happened once or twice a year, that some little man in overalls had just absent-mindedly pulled out the one plug on which the rest of the system depended—and for all we knew, or know now for that matter, it might as well have been that simple and stupid. For we had always been assured that no such thing could ever really happen, and even if we hadn't been assured we'd have gone on assuming it couldn't, simply because—well, because it couldn't. And when it did," he added with a touch of vehemence, "one of the things that happened was that our way of finding out what had happened vanished along with everything else."

With this he entered, in a different tone, on what seemed to be for him the noblest and loftiest and most sorrowful part of memory. No longer stopping to explain, he spoke of the wonders and the terrors that ensued: the giant aircraft cruising over a land suddenly become dark and incapable of giving direction; the few islands of light from self-contained emergency systems; the liners out at sea, themselves such systems, glittering with self-generated brilliance that made them proudly and pathetically independent for a time; the portable radios that answered their worshippers' questions only with static; the dark and cooling houses; the car head-lights beamed into the living rooms all night and fading before the dawn; the cold realization, disbelieved for days but gradually and relentlessly imposing itself upon belief.

"If there was one thing about that time more tragic than the rest," he said, "or so I've heard, for I'm not sure I remember any such thing myself, it was that once, a few days later, everything came on again. Came on with a great, silent rush. But we had left every switch we had, all of us, in the on position—so that we'd know at once, you see—and it seems, or so they say, that by this folly we sucked the power out of the system faster than it could deliver, so fast that in five minutes it failed again and was gone, who knows, forever. All we could do, all we can do, is wait. And though I realize that though some of this sounds like a fairy tale to the younger of you, the whole point of the story, of telling the story every year on the day, is that we are waiting still. That TV set over there is on right now, and it will stay on while we live, in memory and hope. For we believe that what has gone must one day return."

"But why didn't they start all over making the electricity work?" asked one of the older boys. The grandfather looked at him earnestly, and took his time about replying.

"I can't say for certain," he began in an impressively careful way, "that nothing of the sort was ever done. If it was, it either didn't work or else it just hasn't reached this region yet. Think for a moment, young man, of the magnificence of what it was we lost in a moment of time. People accustomed to having such powers in their hands are proud, too proud to fly Ben Franklin's kite again, as the saying is. We have another saying hereabouts, as well: if a king is accidentally locked out of his castle he doesn't build a hovel with his hands. He waits."

There was a silence, possibly of emotion on the old man's side, likely of some small embarrassment in other parts of the room. Perhaps it was to get them past the moment that the grandmother broke in once again:

"You haven't told them about the telephones," she reminded him.

"O yes," the old man said, brightening, "the telephones. They were the strangest things of all, because in the middle of the general panic and blackness and stillness they went on working. They worked for quite a while, I don't know why any more than I know why they finally faded and went dead."

The grandmother patiently said, "You haven't told them yet what telephones were." And the old man told the children what he could about that. He pointed to a telephone on a table back in the shadows, he explained how by turning that little wheel seven different times you could talk to anyone in town you wanted to; how in fact with different combinations of numbers you could talk to anyone in the whole world.

"What did you say to them?" a child wanted to know.

"What did you say to them?" This made the grandfather a little indignant. "Why, the same things you'd say to—to anyone in the world. Hello, how are you, and whatever else you wanted to know, that's what you said to them."

"But it all got strange," he continued. "Even while the telephones were still working, I can remember, the voices at the other end seemed to be getting weaker all the time. You had to shout, and get the other person to shout, to be understood. And after that it got even more uncertain. You'd often feel—it's hard to express it, but you'd often feel the other person wasn't really any longer the person you meant to talk to at all, but someone else entirely. People said very strange things anyhow, in those days, but especially on the phone. We were all so lonely, you see, especially at night, and as often as not you'd pick up the phone when it rang and you'd just hear somebody crying or saying Help me, please help me, but there wouldn't be anything you could do about it if they wouldn't say who they were or where or what kind of help they needed.

"Once in a great while," he added, "you do still hear of people picking up a phone and getting a response, but it doesn't seem to be in a language they understand."

During all this a little boy had crept over and picked up the phone.

"It sounds like the wind," he said, holding it correctly to his ear, "like the wind blowing down a dark tunnel."

"You'd better put that down, son," said a grown-up. "It's not a thing for kids to play with."

"Well," said the grandfather, "of course there's more, there's much more. You children will read about it when you're older, about the sufferings and so on, about that first winter without. I've just given you the bare outline, and why we tell the story every year, which is to pass on to you the memory and the hope.

"But why didn't they ever fix it?" the older boy insisted. And the grandfather looked at him solemnly, rather sternly.

"They just didn't, is all," he said at last. "If they had done I wouldn't be telling you all this, now, would I?"

"But who is They?"

"That is a good question, young man," the elder replied, "and one day, when you're full grown, you may be the one to find the answer. Who knows, you may be the one to find the switch, wherever it is, and turn it on. Stranger things have happened in the world. Meanwhile, I've told you the story, as I was bound to do. I didn't say I could answer every question that might come up. I'm tired, too. And it's time for children to be thinking about bed. Under the covers is the only place children can be safe during the hours of darkness."

Which frightened some and tickled others among the children; one of whom, before falling asleep, expressed the sense of the meeting as it had come through to her:

"It's a funny kind of story," she said, "funny ha ha and funny peculiar both, only I don't know if you're supposed to believe it like Jesus or like Santa Claus."

The Executive

MR BUDBY was the branch manager of the supermarket, and a solid sort of person altogether. In the old days you would not have thought of your neighborhood grocer or butcher as quite up there in the middle class; he belonged on the anomalous dim border between that class and the out-right *worker;* him with his white apron and his straw hat, costume having so much to do with these things. But Mr Budby had definitely made it; although he wore a white coat, if not a straw hat (no hat, in fact), and kept a pencil behind one ear, his connection with a great chain of supermarkets all over the East supplied him with mystery and status beyond what was personally visible; he was an executive, and had that busy air of urgency and constant, delicate calculation. He was an executive, that is, according to the same terminological change that made superintendents out of janitors, morticians out of undertakers, and lubritoria out of gas stations; for that is the way things are with us.

Mr Budby, to look at him more personally, was a stout, perspiring, fussy and authoritarian man, respectful to policemen, local businessmen, and his superiors when they visited, but somewhat intolerable to those placed beneath him in the hierarchy of the supermarket and in the nature of things, which Mr Budby did not question ever.

When Mr Budby and Mrs Budby and the three small Budbys went to church on Sunday morning, it was a wonderful sight! Clean and polished and grave, they came stepping from the clean and polished Ford station wagon, and in order, smallest first and Budby himself at the rear, entered the holy edifice. But why am I making such a fuss? It was not such a wonderful sight at all; it was very ordinary and even a touch depressing. Mr Budby wore black shoes, with very thick, inflexible soles.

Mr Budby had a stock boy named Hubert at the super-market, and this stock boy was what you might call his *bête noire*. You might have called him that, I mean, if you were indelicate, because Hubert was in fact a Negro, and in this phrase we not only don't have integration as yet, but not even separate but equal; for nobody ever gets called anyone's *bête blanche*. Say rather, to find another grand old phrase, that Hubert was *the bane* of Mr Budby's *existence*.

The bane of a man's existence can come in handy in a number of ways, and Mr Budby had found several of these. That Hubert was a Negro, for instance, afforded Mr Budby, in some moods, the satisfaction of feeling that he did not behave like those people in the South who excluded Negroes from things; he felt that things were integrated, in his branch of the supermarket. In other moods, however, he could feel that keeping Hubert on was a conspicuously charitable act. And in still other moods he could blame Hubert for a good deal that happened around the shop, and berate him severely. Finally, in one mood so far, he had kicked Hubert, not very hard, with the square toe of one of those stiff, black shoes.

It is true that Hubert did things very badly. It was fortu-nate that more and more items came in unbreakable plastic containers, for Hubert broke a good many of those that came in glass. And he left dry cereals out in a rainstorm. And he put things on the shelf in a confused manner, so that when the housewife went for *two* packages of Goofies, the second one to slide down would likely as not be Fussies instead. And Hubert knocked over a great pyramid of bottles of maple syrup, many of which broke. These were after all only mis-takes, and for the most part not serious ones—there was no malice in Hubert—but very disturbing to a man interested in good order and discipline.

When Hubert left two hundred cartons of frozen fish stand-ing in the June sun, Mr Budby became seriously angry. Those cartons were ordered for the families who would be coming in Thursday and Friday for fish, for religious reasons. Now there would not be enough.

Hubert came upon request to the dark little cubicle which Mr Budby used for an office. The two of them were alone. Hubert, small, scrawny, with lovely brown eyes watering, trembled. Mr Budby raged as befitted his nature. He said that this was the end, that this was the last. Hubert might turn in his aprons and collect his pay and go. Out. It was the end.

"You are a fool and a no-good, and you will never amount to anything in this world, and this is the end of you," said Mr Budby.

Hubert, standing there, grew huge, maybe eight or nine feet tall, anyhow so he had to stoop to keep his head under the ceiling. The brightness circling his head hissed and crackled against the ceiling, but did not seem to set it aflame. Dark, downy wings stood out of Hubert's back, and fluttered a bit wildly, maybe because Hubert was still trembling some. Hubert's eyes, behind their limpid brown, flamed like stars, bending upon Mr Budby an icy radiance.

Mr Budby was especially unnerved because, never having thought much of the matter, he had not bothered to imagine such a Being as black. He kept waiting for Hubert to grow pink-skinned, with blue eyes and golden hair; but all that happened was that a blaze of black light, a blazing blackness like the moonlit glimpse of calm waters, continued to glimmer all around Hubert.

Mr Budby knew the etiquette for these things.

He knelt.

"Lord," he whispered. "Hubert. Forgive me. I didn't know."

It looked in a way as if Hubert hadn't known either; his features were hard with incomprehension, as if cut from onyx.

"Hubert," said Mr Budby from his kneeling position, "since Thou art so high in the order of the universe, Hubert, how come Thou art not a better stock boy?"

The great wings preened as Hubert shook his shoulders.

"We don't get any training for that," he said sadly.

"What are you going to do to me?" asked Mr Budby.

"Nothing much," said Hubert.

Mr Budby was conscious of a faint disappointment mingled with relief as, released from an awful tension, he fainted.

When he came to, it was evening, with the store closed and himself alone in it.

Mr Budby never told anyone. When Hubert came to work next morning he was the same old Hubert, little, wrong, and apologetically cringing. First thing he did was trip over the wire to the freezer and go on his way, so that the ice cream would have melted if Mr Budby hadn't come along just then and noticed.

"Hubert!" said Mr Budby.

Hubert turned around.

"Dear Lord," said Mr Budby, between oath and reverent address, "Dear Lord, Thou hast pulled the plug on the freezer."

"Yes, sir, Mr Budby, I'm sorry," said Hubert.

Why, he doesn't recall at all, thought Mr Budby. He doesn't have any idea.

"You see it doesn't happen again," he said sternly, shaking his head as he turned away, and adding "Dear Lord" again, just in case.

Probably it never happened, was Mr Budby's thought. But when he went into his cubicle and lifted up his eyes to the ceiling he saw the scorched arc on the Celotex.

"Still and all," he said to himself, "mum's the word." After all, who would believe him? Not even Hubert.

The next week he fired Hubert, though he did it more graciously this time, even adding a small bonus out of his own pocket. There had been no witnesses, after all.

"And anyhow," he added, mainly to himself, "you can't run a supermarket that way."

Bon Bons

AFTER HER HUSBAND left her, Mrs Melisma was able, and in fact compelled, to indulge without restraint her craving for sweets, especially filled chocolates.

Her husband's presence had acted as a moral brake upon this loathsome and delicious appetite, but a brake not always sufficient; the declared reason of his desertion was her having given in once too often to one of her periodic orgies. Not improbably the husband, who would never touch a chocolate, feared the imminent corruption of his own will; and the prospect of their sitting up together amid the litter of box after box of delicate and sticky goo had overcome such love for her as he may have had left, so that he cleared out altogether rather than face it. Perhaps he became a candy addict in another town, I don't know.

But his departure had a very bad effect on Mrs Melisma, who entered on a vicious and tightening circle, wherein grief and guilt demanded to be smothered in indulgence, while indulgence with its terrible aftermath intensified both grief and guilt.

A psychiatrist had told Mrs Melisma, and she believed it, that her inordinate craving for sweet things was the consequence of her having been denied affection in childhood. Sweet chocolate was the symbol and substitute for sweet love. Now that she had lost her husband, this lady proceeded to consume filled chocolates with a reckless, bitter abandonment to despair.

We all of us know too well, and need not repeat in detail, the horrors of enslavement to habit, whether our enslavement be to drugs, food, alcohol, or sex. We know the secret delights, the panicky guilts, the fear of the world's condemnation, or, far worse, its laughter; we know the long and silent colloquies between the reason and the divided will; we know the sickness of self hatred. All of these Mrs Melisma suffered, and no less intensely but perhaps a trifle more because her addiction was so transparently childish in nature, so altogether wanting in the stoical, sometimes tragic dignity which is occasionally found in people who are destroying themselves by drink, narcotics, or gambling—vices which allow them to appear as though they are ruthlessly rejecting the world from above and beyond, rather than from below.

Mrs Melisma, her habit apart, was an intelligent woman, and had been rather an attractive one before it began to be apparent that, with all the other effects of her manner of life, she was gradually burying herself in her own fat. Being intelligent, she did not share one very common superstition of the age, that it is possible to reason oneself out of a bad habit. Not, at least, without running the risk of its being replaced by a worse one; for the habit was a symptom only, while she herself was the disease.

Nonetheless, because she was intelligent, it was not possible for her to resist speculating on just what it was she was doing, or thought she was doing, when she ate all those chocolates. Her speculations began with an exceedingly bold assumption: if I suppose the fault to lie in my own nature, she said, it is obviously incorrigible; science, religion, medicine, psychiatry, have all been helpless. And she proceeded to an equally bold hypothesis (eating chocolates all the while): the fault lies, not in me, but in the external world—and in nothing more likely than in the chocolates themselves.

Now, intelligent or stupid, no one, not a single addict of us all, ever reasons anything out in that way. No, the reasoning, close and elegant in its form, is applied afterward, as a triumphant elaboration of the first beautiful and almost instinctual apprehension of reality. To Mrs Melisma, who had ineffectually consulted all sorts of experts, experts in diet, experts in rational behavior, experts in revealed religion, experts in the secular foundation of ethics, experts in the replacement of one habit with another, and all without success, the first illumination came, poetically, in this way.

"Bon bons," she said aloud, regarding balefully an assortment she knew she was about to open, "you might as well be called mal mals."

She then began to eat, proceeding down the familiar path from pleasure to pain, from brief heaven to the eternally recurrent hell of vomit and disgust; but simultaneously she began to reason.

What was a box of filled chocolates? What was it, not merely in the secret soul, still six years old, of Mary Melisma, but out in the great world, in terrible reality and the luminous heaven of pure idea?

She consulted the great dictionary at first, but upon finding to begin with the absurdly diminutive-sounding invitation: "cf. Nahuatl *chocólatl*", she closed that book in favor of her own experience.

On the first day, before being overcome, she had arrived at one thought: a sweet-tasting outside, with something else inside. It didn't seem much.

But resolution endured, and several days, several boxes, several agonies, afterward, she made a further step: a mystery inside.

This was a real advance, inasmuch as a mystery offered something to be thought about. Thinking, she came to the realization that, despite a great quantity of experience in the field, she was still unable to predict, even about her favorite brand of filled chocolates, the inside of a single one from the outside, either from its shape or from the color of the wrapping paper.

"The unexamined life," she seemed to recollect, "is not worth living."

Inspired, she purchased a pack of filing cards and began, as she ate away, to note down a Descriptive Catalogue of Chocolates, measuring the dimensions and identifying the surface characteristics of each chocolate, and correlating with these both the objective qualities and the subjective sensations communicated to her by the inside. A series of rather odd thoughts began to form itself and emerge from the darkness.

First, the discovery that she did not in fact like the insides of filled chocolates (the outsides had never, perhaps, been a problem; one ate the outsides to reach the insides, and that was all there was to that). What was it, then, that one was eating, liking, requiring, seeking for, in these delicacies?

Was it not mystery itself? Was it not anticipation alone? Was it not precisely the unknown?

The immediate perception of this aroused in her so great a resistance to her new procedures as to make her backslide badly for a week or so; if ignorance alone were horribly to be bliss, she would be ignorant again. But it was as though the serpent of knowledge had taken a prior bite of each piece, and was stronger than the happiness which depended upon the illusory uniqueness of each experience. She resumed her note-taking.

There followed shortly afterward a decisive advance. This involved the observation that boxes of filled chocolates came in layers, two or three or four as the case might be, and that these layers duplicated one another in their arrangement of pieces.

Mrs Melisma had always been vaguely aware that this was so. But bringing the fact into consciousness made possible the invention of a new procedure. Instead of eating one layer completely and going on down to the next, might not one, with the aid of the Descriptive Catalogue, eat, as it were, the same chocolate two, three, or four times in a row, before dealing with the next chocolate, or species of chocolate, in the same manner? She did this, and was appalled as well as enlightened. By even the first repetition, in this new sequence, the novelty of experience had vanished, and by the third anticipation became a mere neutral watchfulness, and by the fourth even this had changed into a species of intellectual contempt.

We do not detail the physical and psychological accompaniment to these experiments, only remarking that Mrs Melisma had become the passionate scientist of her vice, the doctor who contracts the disease he studies to test his observation; save that here the order of events was the reverse of that. One is reminded of De Quincy patiently anatomizing the nightmares of his addiction.

For the discovery of her actual dislike for filled chocolates did not permit Mrs Melisma to stop eating them; it only reduced, and at last removed, the pitiful pleasure which she had obtained before.

She perceived, in effect, that what she ate was not chocolate at all, but only anticipation, suspense; she was eating, as much as anything, not the chocolates themselves, but only the moment between one and the next; now, what did that moment taste of?

Nothing. It tasted of nothing at all. Mrs Melisma wept.

She saw that life had embarked her on a hopeless quest for the One Supreme filled chocolate, containing in itself not the abstract or mere quintessence but the entire luscious being of the absolute; in the search for which all actual experience fell into the gullet and abyss of non-being, and was as nothing.

Nor would the Platonic Idea of that chocolate satisfy; no, it must be the real thing, the filled chocolate incarnate, and to eat it would be to redeem time. That would be the chocolate of which Faust said "let not this chocolate pass away", whereon his bargain with the Devil ended, and he died.

That is as far as it goes, this sad anecdote of Mrs Melisma's addiction. Her realization that she was eating, under a thin coating of negligible chocolate, pure time, the absolutely unmemorable content of instant after instant, tasteless though filling to satiation and disgust, put a stop to her researches; except as these were secretly completed, if that is the word, by a dream she had—

In which she saw the jungles, and, beside the jungles, the sugar cane in fields, the plantations of nougat and almond, the herds of cows giving their milk to be turned into fondant; she saw the black men and the brown men, naked to the waist, going among the trees and through the fields where lonely white men stood with rifles; she saw the great white ships riding, she saw the mumbling stainless steel factories from whose monotonous and automated ruminations a myriad moments of chocolate filled with mysterious sweetness came forth—endless they seemed—; and she saw the candy shops, with their cloying smells and their attendants dressed like nurses in starched uniforms; and she saw by miracle in a million rooms the lonely hunger that existed for the sweetness of life, that sweat and starvation and cold-eyed greed equally and helplessly competed for; and somewhere in all this a child sat, a monstrously chubby child with open mouth, who stretched out pudgy hands before him while he blubbered for the agonizing beauty of this world.

The Mudras of Meetings

WITH ALL the inexpensive Buddhism there is about nowadays, everyone ought to know what is meant by a *mudra*. But there is always a good deal of ignorance about, too, so I shall say briefly that a *mudra* is a gesture of the hand, a position of the fingers, which has a significance. Originally, my authorities tell me, there were only a few *mudras*, each of them significant of a particular event in the life of the Buddha; but in later times the possibilities of this language of the hand were greatly expanded, and there began to be *mudras* for almost everything. These are recorded in the painting and sculpture of India, and interpreted in the religious teachings of India.

I bring the subject up because recent investigations convince me that a similar idiom is arising in the West, which has not yet received the scholarly attention it merits.

I do not mean, of course, the activity which was generally covered by the phrase "talking with one's hands," and which is nowadays tacitly assumed to have been so vulgar, and such a mark of illiteracy, practised only by first-generation immigrants, that it died out some time ago. That sort of thing, I agree, commonly amounted to no more than a good deal of excitable armwaving, and is of no intellectual interest (except as it may belong to the primitive history of our subject) because the armwaving did not signify anything *in particular;* it was mere phatic communion, expressive of a wide and indeterminate range of feelings, and thus could not be recorded in a dictionary.

A more developed form demands a moment's attention. Singers of grand opera have a few conventional gestures invariant at certain places in their performance; I shall give three examples:

a. One arm flung wide, palm outward, expresses geniality,

generosity, magnificence (Don Giovanni inviting the peasants to hot chocolate and coffee at his expense).

b. Slapping oneself on the breast. This has various degrees of intensity, or intonations, ranging from the identification of oneself (Figaro) through proclamations of innocence and shocked surprise at being accused (Radames) to dark pride (Sparafucile). But if the slap strikes the forehead (Simone Boccanegra, Boris) its meaning is unequivocally disaster.

c. Both arms flung wide, palms outward. May mean "Who, me?" but more usually denotes the end of an aria.

But it will be apparent at once that these are not true *mudras* because they express attitudes rather than more or less exact words and phrases.

The place to study this rapidly developing language is the Committee Meeting. My own researches have been conducted in the academic world, but there is nothing to indicate that things are different in business or government, and such evidence as casually comes my way (panel discussions on TV, for example) suggests that it is everywhere the same, potentially a universal idiom.

Please observe in what follows that my examples differ from true *mudras* only in being accompanied—for the most part—by speech. But will this always be true? On the contrary, I am suggesting that the *mudra* is gradually, over a wide area of language, usurping the place of speech and, to a certain rather large extent, of thought as well. I shall try to show that many *mudras* have reached the point of being conventionalized ideographs, whose meaning everyone believes he understands without the words which still accompany the gestures; also that certain *mudras* already have replaced speech, in the sense that they enable the performer to conclude his argument without having ever put his meaning into words.

I recently attended the meeting of a faculty committee

whose purpose I need not tell you; my point being that *mudras* in their present form are verbs, and phrases built around verbs, signifying certain sorts of action and thought— that is, they will be invariant whatever the committee believes itself to be discussing. I may add that I was largely silent on this occasion, being a little stunned at the magnitude of my discovery and consequently too busy observing to give the committee, by word and gesture, my own arguments.

The chairman spread his arms, hands palm down on the table. This clearly meant we were beginning. If there has been undue conversation among the members, this gesture is a little clarified, or emphasized, with a slight sigh. He then spoke more or less as follows; I shall give the accompanying *mudra* as he goes:

At this preliminary meeting, he told us, all we could hope to do was get some overall picture of the subject. To get an overall picture of the subject: an arching gesture outward with both hands, palms down. If we could put our problems into focus (both hands cupped near the eyes, moved in and out several times), we might then *possibly* (slight movement of the shoulders, more a tic than a shrug) formulate the best approaches (this is done as in putting problems into focus, save that the cupped hands are not at eye-level but down near the table, and closer together, and are moved more decisively, as in an abortive move to catch a fly) and delegate various duties to various members (one hand shaken several times around the table, the fingers relaxed but not limp; the same *mudra* with limp fingers denotes unnecessary counting).

A member raised his hand. Now this is a call for attention, and thus perhaps too primitive to be a *mudra*. But note that there are many ways of making it, indicative of as many tones, from the crudely strained gesture of the schoolboy wanting to leave the room all the way to the gesture of this committee member: arm crooked at the elbow so that the hand is close in at shoulder level; index finger and thumb separate by about an inch; index finger separated from the other fingers by the same; all fingers slightly curved; the whole ensemble shaking a little, rather wearily than with anxiety. This is the *mudra* of a master, and you must not expect to command it easily. To all of us in the room it expressed—quite without words!—the following: "Why should we fool around with all these preliminaries? I am here, and in perfect command of the issues at stake. I am ready to present a brief, reasoned account of what we are here for and what we should do in order to solve our problems expeditiously and go home. On the other hand, I know that my colleagues are largely fools, and I believe the chairman to be among the largest fools of my acquaintance; therefore it is probable he will not hear me. I therefore signify in my gesture that I know wisdom is badly treated at such meetings as this, and that, without putting myself forward, I sit here ready to put things right just as soon as the hoi polloi have made their speeches and bewildered themselves into silence."

A *mudra* of that sort is remarkably expressive. The chairman quickly—immediately—was aware of what was being said, and without a word pointed a finger and jabbed it in the direction of the committee member—saying, in effect: "I am a decisive man, I am in authority here, which means I am responsible for suffering fools gladly, and you need not imagine anything you have to say is going to get us out of here before six."

The committee member who had been given the floor now began to speak. His diagnosis was not without its interest. He had, he said, studied this problem with one committee after another (elbow on the table, a limp throw of one hand and its return, several times, as if playing an extremely short yo-yo); we should remember that he had been here for many years (same gesture as before, but made only once, and more largely, indicating finality, disgust, and an indefinite number of years), and if we wanted to go right to the heart of the matter (fingers bunched, pointed forward, a small striking gesture as of a cobra's head lancing forward), we should give him our attention (index finger raised, still).

The trouble had always been, he said, that the matter under study was dispersed among various departments (both hands, parallel, outlined in the air a number of boxes—a sort of table of disorganization), whereas the subject properly ought to be one (fingers brought together near the thumb, hand shaken rapidly as though quivering with indignation) and integrated with the rest of the curriculum (fingers in the same position, strike the points of them decisively, and only once, into the palm of the other hand; allow to quiver as before). Then we should see, he said, how things meshed (fingers interlaced, hold the hands before the chest and bend them against the knuckles until they tremble, making the other members believe that the force of your conviction is so great you are ready to snap off your fingers one by one).

Another member now interrupted. That was all very well, he said (one hand, palm open, is waved outward about six inches and definitely brought to a halt there, indicating certain limits on the approval being granted), it was all very well, but what we really wanted was a clear view of the future (a beautiful *mudra:* the blade of the hand is brought up so that the thumb touches the nose, the hand being parallel with the plane of the nose; then the whole arm is moved forward and backward, rather slowly, several times; if the eyes, with an expression of stern determination, are kept focused at infinity—not on the hand!—they will not cross).

I think it is unnecessary to go any further with this committee meeting. It is clear that its gestures, and such ideas as its members have so far sought to express, duplicate one another more or less exactly, and that the spoken word has for this group of men only a reliquary significance; without it, their understanding might even be improved, and their disagreements at least silenced; while the work of their committee, which has the simple object of keeping them occupied, will go forward undisturbed.

Unbelievable Characters

IT WAS a Sunday afternoon in the late fall. I had come home from college for the weekend, and now, after a heavy dinner, I stood out on the lawn in the last of the good weather, raking the last of the leaves and burning them on the gravel drive. My father had gone up for a nap, my mother and her brother, Uncle Snevely, were still sitting with their second and subsequent cups of coffee. It was a brilliant day, blue and gold, with the heat of noon just beginning to chill as the shadows of the spruces lengthened on the grass; and there was no wind, so that the smoke from the burning leaves, after its first flame and fuss, rose straight up, gray, blue, black, like a signal fire, dissolving overhead.

When I first noticed the skywriter, he was just rounding off the B in ROB and was lazily turning away from his work, really in order to start his run up on the next letter, but a little as if he were a painter standing back from the easel for a critical look. At first I thought he was going to spell my name, which is Robert; then I thought perhaps he was going to spell out, over the suburbs and the city, some tremendous instruction: ROB — BURN — MURDER. I leaned on the rake to watch. But of course the tines of the rake simply bent under at that, so I more or less pretended to be leaning on the rake, while the skywriter completed the word: ROBIN. The "I" had a little kink halfway; he might have stopped to scratch himself, or his knee might simply have straightened and caused him to kick the rudder bar.

Just about then Mother and Uncle Snevely came out on the terrace and sat down a few feet away. It had been such a mild fall that the garden furniture was still out, though the cushions had been removed, and the iron chairs looked old and naked, like the trees.

"I can't resist the smell of burning leaves," said Mother. "I think of when I was a little girl."

"We used to bury each other in the leaves," Uncle Snevely said. "Like the Babes in the Wood." After a moment he added, "It might have been better for me if." And he stopped. Not that his sentence trailed off; no, it definitely stopped. That was Uncle Snevely's way. He had to get it in that he was a failure and realized it, but that he was not going to say any more of it unless invited to, because he wanted you to know that *he* knew he was a bore as well as a failure, and that the one depended on the other, and that he had some dignity left.

"Oh, now, Snevely," said Mother.

I called their attention to the skywriter, who had now got as far as ROBIN HOO, which was already enough to solve the mystery of what he was about: an ad for Robin Hood bread.

"It's awfully beautiful," said Mother. "Even an ordinary little ad can be beautiful sometimes."

Especially, I thought, if you write the ordinary little ad across several miles of sky.

"If you call that skywriting," said Uncle Snevely, "it's pretty plain you've never seen skywriting, that's all."

No one picked this up, which was not a rare thing with Uncle Snevely's openings, and we all watched the tiny black cross in the sky, the buzzing pen-nib, roll leisurely toward the completion of its message. It was beautiful, after all, the white solid jet of smoke, its edges struck to gold and black by the sun and shadow, streaming away in such a definite line; and there was always the millionth chance, too, I suppose, that this time the airplane was really on fire, that the smoke would turn black and begin to plunge away down the sky.

"Oh, look," cried Mother. "He's misspelled bread. Bred."

"It's just another advertising trick," I said. "Though the way people brutalize the language these days, spelling through

t-h-r-u and night n-i-t-e. . . ." I let it go, not only because the others weren't listening, but because I was just
repeating a notion my English teacher had a sort of fix about,
and I didn't care one way or the other what people did with
the language.

Sure enough, the cute little man in the plane came back and
put a caret between the E and the D, and then put an A up
above. The suspense was over, though I didn't really imagine
all the eager spellers on the ground rushing forth to buy
Robin Hood bread as a result.

"The finest man I ever knew was a skywriter," said Uncle
Snevely. "A *chevalier sans peur et sans reproche.*"

I did my best to pretend that some leaves wanted raking
thirty or forty feet away, but Mother said:

"I think you've done enough for now, Robert. Come sit
down and talk with us."

This meant come sit down and listen to us, but there was no
easy way out, so I did.

"Robert will be interested in this story," said Uncle
Snevely, "since he is so interested in aviation."

It was true that I wanted to fly, and intended to join the Air
Force after college—I never did, by the way—but it did not
follow that I was interested in anything Uncle Snevely had to
say. The odd truth was that I was a little frightened of him.

I don't mean being afraid of anything he might do or say to
me, because he was a very mild, maybe even helpless, little
man, who had never been good for anything in his life and
never would be good for anything, and was a drinker as well.
I was frightened of his sadness, his general air of inadequacy,
something awful and weepy about him which I identified
with the smell on his breath and the constant liquid fullness
in his eyes. I had high ideals for myself and had put in all
this time reading good books and preparing myself for cit-
izenship in the community, and I didn't want to run the

risk of catching whatever it was that Uncle Snevely had.

He was a drinker, this was understood, but even about his vice there was something crippled. He wasn't a drunk, he didn't even on any occasion that I remember *get* drunk. Simply, he had to have that sort of nourishment constantly handy if he was to get through the day. When he visited us, which he did for about two to three weeks each fall and spring, he always had some kind of glass within reach. From five o'clock on this would be cocktail or highball; we weren't by any means a nondrinking family, except for me, and I had sometimes, though rarely, seen my father in a condition to which Uncle Snevely probably could not have attained. But with Snevely the stuff was like insulin to a diabetic; he didn't need much of it at a time, but if he needed little he needed it often. And because he wanted so much, at the same time, to be at least reasonably respectable, perhaps even because he thought, poor helpless man, of setting me a good example, his drinking through the morning and afternoon was carried on under a variety of disguises. He would carry a glass of milk through the house, sipping a bit wherever he stopped to chat or read the paper, and the milk would have, say, rum in it. He would go for a glass of water—"Got a frog in me throat," he would say, apologetically and cheerfully— and stop in the pantry on his way back to put gin in the water. Gin, being colorless, was of course a great help to him, but he didn't rely altogether on that; his coffee after lunch, for instance, would have had whiskey in it. And I remember how one afternoon the year before, when I'd come in hot from playing tennis, I saw this half-empty bottle of Coke on the coffee table in the living room and I drank it down, finishing just as Uncle Snevely came back. He looked at me, and he looked at the empty bottle, and then marched straight on through as if that had nothing to do with him. I didn't notice anything except a slightly odd taste till I got upstairs and lay down for a few minutes to rest before taking my shower, and slept through supper.

Right now, on the flagstones beside his right foot, there was a glass of rather thick and viscous-looking water. Moreover, having a cold, he came provided with a pocket atomizer, which, I had maintained to my parents the night before, blew Scotch mist into his nostrils. My father had laughed a little at this, but Mother had become very reserved:

"I don't consider that a very nice joke at all," she had said.

"I wasn't joking," I said.

"It is not a remark for a young man to make about his elders," Mother replied. "You don't know everything about the world yet, you know. My brother has had a good deal of trouble in his time."

What this great deal of trouble was I never knew, but had heard of one, possibly the last, episode in it: Uncle Snevely, only a few years before, had forged a check in somebody else's name and been arrested. My father had persuaded the other person not to prosecute.

Sitting on the terrace, as Uncle Snevely began telling about his skywriter friend, I had a sort of vision of Uncle Snevely sitting at a desk somewhere—in some abstract cloud chamber of my imagination—laboriously, blatantly, and with a glass of gin beside him, forging that check. Of course he would do it badly; of course he would be caught.

The skywriter had begun on Robin Hood bread again, in another part of the sky. His first effort, meanwhile, had already blurred and become illegible.

"There was this fellow, when I was young and lived in New Jersey," said Uncle Snevely, "this fellow used to fly over, every calm day, from the airport at Teterboro, in a little old biplane he'd fly over, to practice his skywriting. And by skywriting I really mean *writing*. Not like this stuff—" he gestured on high—"which is nothing but printing, such as kids do in second grade.

"You are a young man, Robert, and because of all the wonderful things, the inventions, that have come into the world in the few years since you were born, you probably believe in Universal Progress."

"Well, no, as a matter of fact—" I began.

"But Progress is not, um, equal in all directions at once," continued Uncle Snevely, "and in the art of skywriting you might say there has been no progress at all, but actually Regress. In fact, skywriting, which used to be quite a big thing and attracted international attention, is now, you might really say, extinct, a lost art, like stained glass and mummies and, um, things of that nature. Mind you, I am not against Progress."

At this moment we observed, as though it had been summoned by the mention of progress, a jet plane drawing its double chalkline up the sky.

"When I see that, for instance," said Uncle Snevely, pulling with "for instance" the jet plane smoothly into his discourse, "I always see a Great Hand with an Eraser coming after it through the sky. That Great Hand is a Symbol."

He sniffed, took out the atomizer, squirted some whatever-it-was into each nostril, took a sip of gelid-looking water, and resumed.

"I can well remember the first day we saw the skywriter," he said. "One of those long, still, seemingly endless summer days without wind, when, in that small manufacturing town out in the Jersey flats, the heavy air seemed like a kind of eternity, which would never move away, never be replaced by anything fresher—an eternity compounded of smells, smells, or even stinks, which I can understand might be offensive to someone passing though, but in which someone born and bred there, like myself, became a connoisseur: there was the smell of garbage, pig food; the smell of rusting iron in the sun's heat; the smell of decaying rubber tires; and, as the broth in which these ingredients could be picked out, the

faint smell of the salt ocean and the drying mud at low water
—all these were beautifully, yes, beautifully, blended into one
dear essence. Forgive me, Robert—I'm sure your mother
understands. It was, after all, the place of my boyhood and
youth."

I looked at him, and his eyes, sure enough, were overflowing, as they so easily did. Even ordinarily, the eyeballs seemed
to float in a medium which I thought of as made out of tears
and alcohol, which would seep out on very little provocation
and run down his flat cheeks.

"It was on such a day, toward the end of summer, that we
looked out the office window and first saw the skywriter. I
was, by the way, as a young man, more, um, serious than I
may seem to be now, I had ideals and ambitions and industry
and a certain amount of brains to go with 'em. I worked in
the biggest of the local factories, a place which made the old
Triplex typewriter—they went under in the crash, in Twenty-
nine—and I had already got to be assistant to the manager of
the ribbon division.

"By the time we noticed him, this skywriter had already
drawn three parallel lines across the air, and was beginning
what you might call his penmanship exercises—*e's, l's* and
o's—for the day. They used to have not only a better grade of
smoke, back there, one which lasted longer, at least in still air,
and didn't spread out as though you were writing on blotting
paper, but also the airplane itself, for some reason I have never
understood, was a handier instrument, and the device for
squirting the smoke made a finer nib than they use now."

"Those old airplanes," I said, "were more maneuverable,
because they were slower. A medium turn, in a jet, would
take you over six miles of sky."

"I suppose there is some such reason for it," Uncle Snevely
said. "Anyhow, this old biplane seemed just right for the
purpose, and everyone in the office, as I suppose most everyone all over town, watched with great attention while the

fellow finished his practice warm-up and then wrote out in Copperplate style: *A thing of beauty is a joy forever*, and *Beauty is Truth; Truth Beauty, that is* . . . But there, it seemed, he ran out of ink, or smoke, and flew away to the east, leaving behind him those noble thoughts so neatly written across the sky, words which remained there through the afternoon in scarcely dissolving strokes, until they were outlined in bold relief by the rays of the late sun at evening. We had all been severely told to get back to our desks, but the thing had captured our imaginations, and I especially kept raising my head every few minutes to stare at those majestic messages, which seemed to stir in me what I may well call a divine discontent, not only with the ribbon division and my assistantship, but also with the idea and the whole life implied in those things."

"I don't remember any skywriter like *that*," Mother said, not in contradiction but rather wistfully.

"One forgets, one forgets—so much," answered Uncle Snevely. "That may have been the year we thought you had tuberculosis, and you spent the summer in the Adirondacks, remember that?"

"Well," said Mother, "I do remember about the TB scare, and the Adirondacks, but surely I was never away the whole summer?"

"Well, anyhow," continued Uncle Snevely, "he was there, after that first time, nearly every day—every clear day without wind, of which there were a good many. He would write, most days, beautifully turned sentences, like, *To be or not to be, that is the question* and *Shall I compare thee to a summer's day?*, but on other days he would write down, or write up if you like, more puzzling things, sometimes things which were perhaps not altogether in good taste, such as *Conception is a blessing*, or *Don't laugh, lady, your daughter may be inside*. Once there hung over our heads for the whole afternoon the ominous symbols $E = mc^2$, the sense of which we of course were unable to make out, and he sometimes wrote in Latin, using an elegant uncial style: *Flectere si nequeo superos, Acheronta movebo.*

"I was courting at this time a young lady, Eunice Brown by name, who was a little above me socially, being the daughter of the manager of the ribbon division. I communicated to Eunice something of the emotions in me which were stirred up by those writings in the sky, she acknowledged similar stirrings in herself, and we wondered together if it might not be possible for us to meet the person responsible for so arousing us, and perhaps get him to write for Eunice and myself something from Edna St. Vincent Millay or Elinor Wylie.

"But at the same time, being an alert young fellow, I thought I saw a way to combine business and pleasure here. I suggested to Mr Brown, who in turn suggested it to the front office, that this skywriter, if he could be persuaded to it, might write advertisements for the Triplex typewriter all over the sky above New York City, which would be an original, attractive and inexpensive means of reaching the greatest (and greatest typewriter-using) population in the world. This notion of mine, though it was Brown's notion by the time it reached the heights where policy was decided, found favor in the eyes of the mighty, and Brown's gratitude was enough to make me, as I had hoped, the delegate.

"So you may imagine not only my pleasure but my vanity as Eunice and I drove over to Teterboro; with a few words I had achieved so many things—a day off, with my young lady beside me, in her father's Pierce-Arrow with the top down, a day off which, moreover, actually bettered my reputation in the company whose representative I was; and, with all those things, the gratification of my private desire to become acquainted with the skywriter and know something of his art. I even imagined, as we drove along, a scene in which a lean young hero of the air offered me free flying

lessons, on account of my great interest, and showed a willing-
ness to accept me as his first pupil. The world seemed to
open out, although at the same time my reason told me that
at best I should approach no closer to this ideal than perhaps
being allowed to compose the ads which the skywriter would
weave the words of over New York City, before an audience
of millions.

"Eunice was less aware than I of the complexity of motives
involved in our visit; she had brought along a volume of
Edna St. Vincent Millay, and was trying to decide on a
favorite passage short enough to be performed by airplane.

"Romantic dreams," said Uncle Snevely, taking a new tone
and interrupting himself as it were, "romantic dreams, I have
always found, come true and not true in curious ways. Sometimes I think that on the drive over I should have paid more
attention to what Eunice was thinking, and less to what I was
thinking. They fell in love, Eunice and this man. Nelson St.
Yves was his romantic name.

"And of course—of course," Uncle Snevely added, in
what was for him a ferocious voice, "he turned out to be
short and fat, and nearly forty years old, and in every way
unsuitable except for, I guess, his most romantic name of
Nelson St. Yves."

I may point out here that Uncle Snevely, even as a youth,
could not have been strikingly the opposite of short and fat.

"He stood by his very dirty airplane, one of those left over
from the First World War, the kind they called Jennies—"

"The Curtiss JN-4."

"Yes, I suppose its name was something like that. Anyhow,
he was smoking a cigar, right next to the engine; he kept the
cigar in his mouth even while he leaned in under the cowling
to fiddle with things, wires and such, and he talked around
the cigar with a kind of tired affability, a take-it-or-leave-it
attitude which somewhat angered me, nervous as I was in the
first place on account of the danger of fire or an explosion.

After all, we had come all that way to be nice to him, and he seemed to be taking it as his due, the way a king would. But I suppose what I was feeling, what caused my irritation, was Mr St. Yves' beginning to take notice of Eunice, and her beginning to respond to him (she was becoming less 'sweet' and more nervous, more what you might describe as a 'modern' young woman) so that I was being treated more or less as an extra.

" 'So it's your neighborhood I've been working over,' said Nelson St. Ives. 'Glad you like the stuff. Some places, people can't put up with it—but they don't really own the sky, do they?' His laugh showed him to have very dirty teeth and many gold fillings.

" 'You write such beautiful thoughts,' said Eunice, 'and you write them beautifully, too. There's something so solemn about living under a sky that has messages on it. Reverend Dyce used your skywriting in his sermon last week,' she added.

" 'Well, that's normal,' the skywriter said. 'Though actually it's not the messages I care about. Most anything would do. It's the style that has to be perfected.'

"This was my chance to get in and say that if the messages didn't matter, why, the Triplex typewriter people were prepared to pay so and so much for him to go and write *their* messages over New York City, in a style as near perfect as he could make it. But Eunice had seen her chance, and taken it first, handing him the Edna St. Vincent Millay book and asking if Mr St. Yves would possibly be so kind. . . .

"He stood there holding the book in his greasy hands.

" 'Sure,' he said. 'Which line do you want me to write?'

"And Eunice, who had been so busy trying to make up her mind on just this one point, now blushed and said, 'Oh, I think you ought to be the one to choose.' And they stood there smiling at each other in a tender and exasperating way.

" 'What will you give me if I pick your favorite line?' he

asked, throwing Eunice into a pretty confusion because the answer obviously was supposed to be 'a kiss' and Eunice was not, or had not been till then, the easy kissing kind. To save her embarrassment I cleared my throat and began.

" 'What the Triplex typewriter people are prepared to give,' I said, and outlined our proposals, which, after seeing Mr St. Yves in person, I had begun to believe were not only fair, but actually more generous than necessary. So using my discretion I offered a sum substantially less than I was em- powered to. He listened quietly, leaning against the lower wing of the plane, chewing at his cigar, and now and then running a hand over his not recently shaven chin.

"When I had finished, he said first that skywriting over a big city like New York was unprofitable—'unprofitable for the style, you get me?'—because of the numerous air pockets which interrupted the steady motion of the plane."

"There are no such things as air pockets," I broke in on Uncle Snevely here. "No one talks of air pockets any more. That's a superstition."

"Well, I am only telling you what the man said to me," Uncle Snevely replied a little huffily. "He said that he prac- ticed out on the flats, over the salt marshes, because there were no, or very few, air pockets there. That's all I know."

"He must have meant convection currents," I said, feeling at the same time that by stooping to the criticism of this detail I implied that in other respects I was ready to believe my uncle's odd and silly story.

"Robert, don't interrupt your uncle," Mother said.

"But the main thing," Uncle Snevely resumed, with a sharp look at me, "was not the, um, convection currents—no, it was more surprising than that.

" 'It's a nice-enough proposition,' said Nelson St. Yves, 'and I could use the few bucks. But, you see, I can't afford to lose my amateur standing; they're very strict about that.' And he went on to explain that his practicing so hard was in preparation for the International Championship Competition in Skywriting, which was going to be held that winter in Oberammergau."

"Snevely," said Mother, "Oberammergau is where they have the Passion Play."

"I'm sure he said Oberammergau," said Uncle Snevely, "but it doesn't matter, really."

"But I've never heard it mentioned in connection with sports," Mother persisted.

"Who's interrupting now?" I said.

"I raised the offer somewhat," said Uncle Snevely, "but rather halfheartedly, not only because I was rather disillusioned with the man, who seemed definitely casual and ill-bred, but because after all his amateur standing was obviously of the first importance to him, and I hadn't come prepared to argue about that.

"It was *all* rather disillusioning. Eunice's father, Mr Brown, was a pretty good man, but strict, and when it turned out that instead of accomplishing something big I had merely been taking a day off on the company's time, at its expense, and in his automobile, not to mention with his daughter, he would not look favorably on me at all, especially since he had sold the whole scheme to the higher-ups as his own. So I was all for getting out of there, and making the best of a bad situation by showing up for work at least half the day. But while I was thinking how to make our excuses politely but definitely, St. Yves and Eunice were getting on fine, chattering about the sky, and flying, and messages, and Edna St. Vincent Millay, whose poetry the man continued to leaf through as they talked.

" 'Why not come and see how it's done?' he said, to her and not to me. I coughed.

" 'You mean—in the airplane?' Eunice was being girlishly delighted, and, I thought, somewhat scared. I coughed, and no one paid me any attention.

" 'Why, I'd be just pleased as anything,' Eunice cried, and then turned to me with a serious face. 'It will be all right, won't it?' she said in a pleading way.

" 'Your father didn't give me permission to let you go up in an airplane,' I said.

" 'Are you her cousin?' asked St. Yves, 'or what?'

" 'Oh, Daddy won't mind,' Eunice declared. 'Come, it'll be fun.'

"In the end, it was obvious to them that they had to take me, since there was just room. The airplane could be flown from either cockpit, and the front one was large enough for two. But this was something I didn't understand until too late. St. Yves suddenly became very polite and helpful to me, and insisted on my climbing up on the wing and thus into the bucket seat, very low, of the after cockpit; he strapped me in, answered my nervous questions—'Parachute? Never use 'em. Too close to the ground'—and showed me how to place my legs and feet to be out of the way of the duplicate set of controls. Then, when I was snugly tied down, and fitted with a dirty old helmet he had handy, he and Eunice climbed into the front cockpit together, with, on his side, much gentlemanly handing of her up and fussing lest her skirt get dirty. I was enraged, but I was also extremely nervous about going up in an airplane for the first time, and before I could settle myself enough to say anything a mechanic arrived to swing the propeller, the engine started with several bangs and a kind of jittery roar, and it was too late.

"That ride," said Uncle Snevely, and paused to take several sips from his glass. "That ride, I tell you, is something I will never forget. That rickety old airplane, for one thing, creaking and groaning, the engine sputtering and sometimes, even, just as we started down, stopping for a moment entirely—"

"Gravity feed," I said wisely.

"Whatever it was. Oh," said Uncle Snevely, "the difference between seeing something from far away and seeing the same thing close up, or for that matter inside it, and not really *seeing* it at all. Dreadful.

"The first part wasn't so bad, just flying over there. And the last part, just flying back, was a blessed relief—but in between, I tell you, I suffered.

"All that had looked so graceful and quiet from the ground, all that carving of immortal thoughts against the great background of the heavens, became, when you were involved, a hell of noise and motion and the smell of oil and whatever it was there was in that smoke he used. St. Yves would throw the airplane violently over on its side, my legs and ribs and even sometimes my head would knock against the cockpit wall; he would rise, and my stomach would sink; he would dive, and my stomach would come up to my chin; for a moment we would hang upside down, then nose over so that the brown marshes and my unrecognizable home town would swim madly up toward us, then suddenly we would be in a turn so intense that my cheeks felt as if they were being pushed down off my face. And, yes, finally, I was sick. I threw up, and could not avoid spattering the trousers of my best suit. But even that wasn't the worst. The worst was that it didn't stop, it went on. Surely, I thought, now that I've been sick it has to be over, there's nothing more can be demanded. But it just went on.

"No, I'm wrong, there was one thing which, at least in memory, was worse than that." Uncle Snevely made this assertion more impressive by drinking again. "That all this time you actually could not see what the man was doing. I presumed we were making letters, since that was what we had been taken up to do; but we were so close to the letters that no impression of the message could be formed whatever. Sometimes, even in my desperate condition, I got the idea that we must be dotting an *i*, or climbing the sickening curve of a *d*. And as I looked down I could see between my knees the stick which in obedience to St. Yve's hand was making us go through these insane contortions. The stick made very small motions this way and that, while we made these enormous motions this way and that. But even after we were through we didn't get a sight of the finished product; our track home kept us end-on to whatever we had written, for, as St. Yves said when we got safely back on the ground, we had been short of gas and couldn't spare the time to stand off and admire the work.

" 'What did we write?' asked Eunice, who seemed not to have suffered at all, but to have enjoyed herself immensely.

" 'Oh, you'll see, it'll still be there when you get home,' St. Yves said carelessly. And then out of somewhere in his flying costume—and this was in Prohibition—he quite openly got out a bottle of whiskey, and offered it around.

"I didn't drink, back then," Uncle Snevely said somewhat severely, eying his glass. "But what with the punishment I had just taken, and with the shock I received when Eunice, with no hesitation whatever, took a strong pull from the unsanitary mouth of that bottle, I felt justified there and then in tasting alcohol for the first time."

Uncle Snevely sat very straight, and seemed to pull round him more firmly the robes of an invisible dignity.

"So that is something else I owe to Nelson St. Yves," he said.

"He does not sound so much like a *chevalier sans peur et sans reproche* to me," said Mother.

"That was the ideal of him which I had formed," said Uncle Snevely. "He embodied the ideal in a reality which I may have found detestable, but that is not to the point. He was a knight of the sky, that was all there was to it, and he did not live, as we do, by earthly rules."

Uncle Snevely was quietly, automatically weeping again, but he went on.

"We drove back pretty much in silence, Eunice and I. I felt humiliated and still sick, and the whiskey which I imagined accusingly on my breath did not help me to recover my spirits at all; whereas Eunice seemed to glow with a quiet but intense happiness, a dreamy quality, as though some simple discovery like flying had all at once given her a new perspective on life, and expanded the limits of her vision.

"Long before reaching home, of course, we saw the results of our afternoon's work, pleasure, torment, however you look at it. In letters made fire by the setting sun it was written across our local heaven that *Euclid alone has looked on Beauty bare*, and by suppertime a good deal of indignation had been generated about it, too. Many people in our community did not like the idea of anyone, even a dead mathematician, looking on beauty bare; misunderstanding the very pure intention of the line in this way, they naturally were disposed to make a fuss about the effect of such a thing on their children's morals.

"Mr Brown said nothing to me, probably because he did not know exactly what there was to say, and before he could make up his mind about that, he—and I—had other troubles. For during that weekend, as he told me on the Monday morning, Eunice had literally 'taken off' with Nelson St. Yves, and nothing was heard of the pair of them for about two months. Mr Brown, it was plain, regarded this as largely my fault, and said that though he did not propose to take any outright action against me, such as having me fired, he would see to it, he said, that there would be no further advancement for me in any firm of which he was a member."

"If that is the end," said Mother, "I think it shows Eunice was not the girl for you, and you were fortunate to find it out in time."

"I'm sorry, Uncle Snevely," I said, "but I just don't believe skywriting was ever the way you make out."

"That's extremely rude to your Uncle Snevely," said Mother.

"It wasn't the end, though," said Uncle Snevely. "Eunice

came back and I married her when she was four months pregnant."

"Snevely!" cried Mother. "You never!"

"And as for you," said Uncle Snevely to me, "if you don't believe these simple things I have been telling, well, I am sorry for you."

He got out the atomizer again and squirted himself, then he took a long pull from his glass, which was almost empty.

"You won't want to hear about the circumstances of my marriage," he said, "my marriage, which has made me what I am today." He smiled at this pompous phrase, or at something. "She died at childbirth, and the child died, a little boy. I was going to be courageous, and make Eunice be, and call him Nelson. But that wasn't necessary.

"At her funeral he came back. He flew so low I thought he meant to crash at her grave, but his arm showed over the side of the cockpit and he threw some flowers, some lilies, very big ones. Then he went off a bit up the sky and wrote on it, *Sweets to the sweet, Farewell*, and flew off elsewhere. I called the airport at Teterboro, but he had not landed there."

"After all, even if you had found him, what would you have said to him?" I asked.

"I would have killed him," Uncle Snevely said. "I've never told anyone that story until today," he added, picking up his glass and rising. "Thank you both for your patience in listening. The sun's going in now, and I feel a trifle chill. Besides, it must be almost the cocktail hour."

And he padded off up the crazy pavement to the house, turning at the porch door to say, "I would have killed him, it would be kind of you to believe that."

"Of course Snevely never married," Mother said as soon as he had disappeared.

"The whole story is pretty absurd," I said. And when she didn't answer: "You agree, don't you?"

"You mustn't be so cruel as that," said Mother. "It

obviously meant a great deal to him. When you are older, and understand more about the things people go through, the things that happen to them in this world, you will sympathize more readily—however it really happened, it must have been a terrible blow to him."

"However *what* really happened?" I cried, in some excitement. "You say yourself that he never married—there was no Eunice, there was no child, there was no tragedy. And of my own knowledge I can tell you that there never was any such skywriting as that, and that there was no Nelson St. Yves, an obviously fake name if I ever heard of one—"

"And no Teterboro, New Jersey, either, I suppose?" Mother said this with some spirit.

Then, as she arose and followed Uncle Snevely into the house, she said with her regained gentleness, "There is always something, Robert, always."

Uncle Snevely died that year, in the winter. He had been living in a furnished room in a town some two hundred miles away from us, and evidently having for once got thoroughly drunk he must have become incompetent to get back to that room, for he was found the next day in a snowdrift. Among his papers, which came to Mother, there was a picture of a girl, but no name on it. And at the funeral I rather hoped for an old Jenny to fly over, with a hand emerging to drop maybe a pint of whiskey, but none did; nor were there among the few mourners any strangers who might have been mistaken for Nelson St. Yves.

One thing more. I did write this up the following year for my course in English composition. I may not have phrased it exactly as I have here, but the order of things was pretty much the same. By that time I had given up wanting to be a pilot, and wanted to be a novelist instead, so although I was merely repeating what Uncle Snevely had told me I called the thing "a short story." Professor Selvyn wrote on it as follows (I looked it up just the other day) in his kinky, hurried, erratic hand:

Good beginning effort. Your greatest trouble—apart from your obvious [two words illegible here]—is that you do not create believable characters. All these characters are unbelievable. In rewriting, build up the mother. Make Eunice more believable especially. However, this is a good try; have you thought of printing it in the Blazon *[school literary magazine]? B.*

Below this, as an afterthought, someone else—I never found out who—had scribbled:

Have you noticed: Nelson St. Yves = Snevely + Son + St.?

I had not noticed, and I do not much care, though now that I am older and sympathize more I can see it as a sadly appropriate epitaph for Uncle Snevely that he should finish as one among a group of unbelievable characters.

The Escapist

AFTER THE DIRE and unconvincing nostalgias, the tears un-
heard at night and unacknowledged the next morning,
the repeated threats of "I will not" dedicated in silence to a dead
god whose name was history; after the meaningless atrocities
of pride committed without courage inside the mind and
upon the self; after the pursuit of so numerous apotropaic
rituals; after the weekends with drawn blinds, letting the
clocks run down; after these things and so many years, not
much remained; but these were the things which Mr Morse
had to consider day after day through a stillness broken by
flatulence, itching-and-scratching, and headaches which now
and then audibly buzzed within as though thought were
fumblingly approaching an incarnation.

Doubtless he was merely sick. He slept badly, and that was
a sign of the onset of mental illness. He had been awakened by
nightmares until he was too frightened to sleep. He did not
like being drunk, and he did not like being sober. Probably he
hated life, and this thought scared him because he hated
(feared) death; sometimes he thought of himself as another
person who would turn to him and say "Die, then," "if the
room is smoky, leave it," etc. And he was very much afraid
of this person within, who had never spoken as yet but who
uncontrollably might one day, any day, and who when once
he had spoken would be unanswerable, this rebel, this subver-
sive, this treacherous citizen in the maquis of the self.

It was so unfair. Consider childhood.

Self-pity.

Consider childhood.

One power after another had let him down, the parents,
schools, gods, armies—and he had never been much interested
in money.

A fortune-teller at a carnival had told him "You are without love, you cannot love." The carnival wintered in Florida and in the good weather cruised through New England, riding the children in various exciting circles, giving worthless prizes for meaningless accomplishments, and telling the adults they could not love. "It is all in here," the fortune-teller had said, pointing to the somewhat flat decolletage of her dress, "in here."

The heart, she meant. It was all in the heart. She meant that Mr Morse, having no heart, had nothing in there, and could not love. As though the heart were a teat, running the milk of kindness, the milk and honey of the lost land of Canaan, where the Arabs and the Jews assaulted one another in the name of—in the name of?

But Mr Morse had, of course, a heart. It frightened him most of all, because one day it would stop. Then what?

You walked very carefully, and all the streets were called straight. What difference did that make?

"You should try to take an interest in other things," he said to himself now. "You should try to live, and look outside yourself, not always in. It's unhealthy always to be concerned with the self. Take an interest in the world."

He marched himself smartly to a newsstand half a block away, he bought a paper, he held up the paper before his eyes while people pushed past him taking a tiny moment of their time to express in this way the resentment they felt over his having spread himself so on their sidewalk. He shut his eyes and opened the paper, because the first thing he read would be the important thing.

"The Venus Flytrap is one of over six thousand species of carnivorous plants in the Western Hemisphere."

How terrible! But one must get somehow outside the self. He tried again.

"Pope Offers Code for Fashions: Sanctions Modest 'Adornment of Body'."

Now that was more interesting. You could think about that. It could be argued this way, and argued that way. You could talk about the Middle Ages, for instance, if you knew about the Middle Ages. Mention the relation of clothing to modesty; to warmth; to provocation; clothing as disguise; clothing as symbolism of rank and power.

"Drawing the line between the sinful and the acceptable is hard, but the intentions of both the designer and the wearer are a starting point, the Pope said."

Mr Morse folded the paper into a convenient shape for holding in one hand. He began to walk, reading, reflecting on what he read, and observing his surroundings. A neat man, a trifle rundown but neat, and no troublemaker. People bustled around him rapidly but without resentment now, since he was going somewhere.

It was a street of shops, running in the near-distance into a residential section. Mr Morse passed a five-and-ten, a dress shop called Vanity, Inc., a hardware store, came to a stop at a liquor store, where he regarded for a long moment the pyramided bottles of mostly golden fluids, which caught the light with a splendid purity warranted by labels and government tax stamps; there was a poster also, showing a field of waving grain golden in sunlight under a blue, endless sky. "The Vodka of Free Enterprise," said the caption. "No Unpleasant Aftertaste."

"No messages please, please no messages," muttered Mr Morse. "No symbolism, no embolism. Please." He walked somewhat more rapidly on, applying his nose to the print before him.

"Dress designs should not show off one's physical assets as a source of indiscriminate provocation, but should reserve them to proper occasions and to the wise uses intended by the Creator inside the limits of chastity and modesty."

My God, why hast thou forsaken me? asked Mr Morse.

I was a child, it used to be simple. I do not want to live, I do not want to die, all I was ever trained to want was some modest inbetween arrangement, nothing vital, so and so many haircuts per century, so many trips to the dentist, now and then a new pair of shoes, the newspapers would keep coming out every day, maybe a cigar after dinner. It's not much to ask, I would even brush my teeth.

Another dress shop, this one called Lady Fair. Mr Morse gazed abstractedly at the slender mannequins with their rope eyebrows, remote stares, postures of strained, objectless elegance. They were dressed in cool blues and greens, short-sleeved or no-sleeved summer gowns somewhat loosely cut with a carefree sailor-boy effect to the collars, and their gestures revealed smooth, hairless armpits.

"On the other hand, the Pope said, there was no reason why the dress of young women should not sing of the happy theme of the springtime of life, and help inside the limits of modesty to provide the psychological premises needed for forming new families. This implied that gay though decent clothing for young women, designed to please a young potential bridegroom's fancy, was morally right."

"You are morally right," Mr Morse said to the mannequins, "but be careful." He became aware now of a pair of living eyes looking from the gloom of the shop through the legs of the mannequins. He made out the face of a little old lady, rouged and lipsticked, framed by earrings made of cowrie shells; a fixed smile, like old paint on a splintered board, neither contradicted nor confirmed an equally fixed disapproval, between bewilderment and fear, in the expression round the eyes, which glittered semipreciously in their wrinkled purses.

Like two beasts in their cages, he thought, and spoke aloud:

"I didn't do it, dear. You didn't do it. Even the Pope didn't do it."

And grinned at her; whereat her smile began to share the ferocity of her eyes, and he walked slowly on.

"Mature ages properly look to dignity and serene happiness in their dress, the Pope said."

Mr Morse passed from the line of shops, which somewhat deteriorated at this end, and were liable to have strings of salami hanging in the windows, into the residential section beyond, where trees shaded his thin-haired head although it was not a rich neighborhood. He walked, in this manner, nearly every day, weather permitting, but he was not one of those indefatigable connoisseurs of the architecture of time who note both ruin and renewal and presently are known for walking archives. Mr Morse had little enough interest in history, he simply walked. On bad days he went to the library, or sometimes a movie. People said of him variously and on no particular foundation that he was a scholar or artist, that he was unemployable, that he was crazy, that he had been disappointed in love. It would have been true to say that his feet often hurt. He was a man disappointed in structures of all kinds, and consequently accustomed to digest and excrete his thoughts as he did his food—both were poor—accepting whatever nourishment they helplessly offered the organism on the way through. He did not keep butterflies in glass cases, and would not have catalogued the six thousand species of meat-eating plants.

Mr Morse walked slowly along the dappled street. After the dire and unconvincing nostalgias, the tears, the threats; after the unspeakable takings in and the more unspeakable spittings out; after the pride of life and the lust of the eye and the consequent humiliations of these, the uneffected rejections, implausible reforms, ruthless anxieties which took him by the throat and shook, shook; after these things he walked slowly along, pausing by a schoolyard where children played.

The children played. Mr Morse looked through the fence. No details. He began to cry, not much; or his eyes simply watered with the sunlight on the white concrete, the pride of life and the lust of the eye, the great betrayal.

"Little ones, little ones," he clucked as one holding out peanuts to birds. The children paid no attention, but a policeman did, coming up and saying:

"Trouble, bub?" He used this approach, Mr Morse gathered, because this was civilization and in civilization you did not begin, whatever your suspicions, by accusing a plain middle-aged man of being a pervert or dope-pusher simply because you found him weeping in the street, near children, in the street.

"It's nothing, nothing," he said, and then with a little more force, "nothing," again.

"You'd be going someplace?" the policeman said.

"Out walking, officer."

"You want to rest, there's a park, couple of blocks up."

"Thank you, thank you." Mr Morse was already walking again, though he could not decide whether he was walking away from the policeman or being pushed by him.

"City street's no place to loiter in," the policeman finally said, reminding Mr Morse not ungently of the majesty of the law everywhere around them, that there is in effect a time to be born and a time to die, a time to plant and a time to pluck up that which is planted, and so forth. With this reminder the policeman, a man also in middle-life, fell away from Mr Morse's side as if he had been an escort vessel.

There *was* a park a couple of blocks up, and opposite the park a church, white, wooden, revealing at this distance a somewhat ostentatious New England simplicity but no special denomination. Mr Morse deliberated loosely between God and Nature. He was born a Jew, and once in youth had tried to become a Roman Catholic, though perhaps he had not tried very hard; the priest who had him in hand for the orientation course, or whatever they called it, had openly doubted the sincerity of his motives, the purity of his intention (or whatever they called *that*), and had in a very short way advised him to be more humble.

"To you?" Mr Morse had had spirit back in those days.

But since then he had fallen away, if that was to have approached. He had studied some in Buddhism, but the idea of annihilation, so far as he understood it, frightened him badly (he had also been serious about ideas, back then), and he remembered a phrase about Nirvana, that it represented "a transcendental suicide, not for this time only but forever."

My God, Lord of my mediocrity, Divine Sponsor of my hypocrisy, Creator of this dirt, Mr Morse prayed. Why shouldn't I go in to Thee and fall on my face on the floor and beg Thy forgiveness even if I don't believe in Thee?

And no matter what denomination, he added.

With this intention he crossed the little park.

Just at this moment, from somewhere nearby, a siren went off with a terrible cry.

High noon, thought Mr Morse.

Then other sirens, at greater distances and less, began to go off, and the church bells started to ring somewhat wildly and in no particular tuneful order.

Mr Morse was amazed. For me! he thought, it couldn't be for me? As when the saint came from his exile to be Pope, and all the bells of Rome went off at once, by themselves. Lord, I am not worthy.

There were not many people in the park: a few nursemaids with children in and out of carriages, a few (possibly) bums. But on hearing this racket set up by the sirens and bells they all at once got up, the nurses with all deliberate speed stuffed the infants back in the carriages, or took elder children by the hand, the bums (if they were) folded their newspapers into their pockets, and all moved off.

He knew perfectly well that he was not worthy, and that if the heavens should open upon him a kewpie doll would descend on a string, but he stood there for some moments, staring up the height of the white church before him to the golden steeple which invaded, or more humbly indicated, the endless blue of heaven above.

"Air raid drill, bub." The same officer, having no doubt followed him out of suspicion too dark to be named. "Everybody under cover. Don't stand around." He pointed to the church with his nightstick, while nudging Mr Morse forward. This action, in annoying Mr Morse, changed his mind.

"I was just going into the church, as a matter of fact," he said, putting his face close to the policeman's ear and speaking loudly over the sirens, without, however, shouting. "But now I have changed my mind. I am an American citizen and a free man. If the Bomb falls, I am here."

"Bomb?" The policeman stared at him. "What bomb?" He continued to edge Mr Morse over the street and toward the church door.

"What Bomb?" Mr Morse was equally incredulous. "You don't know?"

"Look, buddy," the officer said gently but in so loud a voice as to cancel most of the gentleness. "There's no bomb, this is a drill, nothing is going to happen, but you have to get off the street, see?"

"Let the trumpet blow," cried Mr Morse, "let the quick and the dead stand up to be counted on the right hand and on the left. Man can die here as well as elsewhere."

Inexorably they were nearing the church. The officer now not merely nudged Mr Morse, but grasped his arm and urged him on.

"This neighborhood has got to be clean five minutes after the alert," he said grimly. "Make trouble for me, bub, and I make trouble for you."

Mr Morse in a moment almost amounting to real violence

was hustled up the lawn of the church, past a sign reading "Togetherness To Pray The American Way," and into the dark vestibule, where it seemed to him that many willing hands accepted him, drew him in, as though in rescue from deadly peril.

"Right downstairs," a cheerful baritone voice was saying. "Everyone downstairs, there's no need for alarm, keep cool everybody, don't crowd on the stairways, there's plenty of room."

Mr Morse, pressed on all sides by what seemed a relatively small number of persons, as in some low-budget movie where a few extras have been told to make like a throng, felt that his arms and legs scarcely belonged to him any more, or to his will. A mystical participation, he thought, lurching downstairs among other bodies: togetherness.

The channel he flowed in presently widened out, and he stood on his own two feet once again, in the cellar beneath the church. Still stumbling a bit, he passed two deal tables where three old ladies sat, and entered an area rather reminding him of his highschool gym, except that it was crowded with people, mostly women, and objects he did not at first identify; but it had the same brown smell of varnish, sweat, and superfluous steam heat.

"Keep calm, everybody," the baritone voice resumed; it seemed to have followed them downstairs. "There's no reason the rummage sale can't go right on, there's room enough for all, and who knows—" it chuckled here "—who knows, our captive audience may find they're glad they came. Prices are clearly marked on every article, friends, you pay the ladies at the tables under the stair."

Now in the light shed at intervals by nude yellow bulbs, and even in the gloom between, Mr Morse was able to perceive that some of the clutter in this place was not made by people but by, as it were, the ghostly hanging headless facsimiles of people, dresses, suits, and overcoats on racks, swaying or shaking with the continuous vibration set up in the floor by the footsteps of the living. Women, mostly, and a few men, toiled studiously through aisles full of this stuff, feeling fabrics, reading price-tags, even in a few instances trying on such items as might naturally be tried on within the limits of modesty.

Aside from all this clothing on hangers, there were some tables piled with fabrics such as sweaters, dish-rags, scarves, blouses, undershirts, socks, and neckties; some areas of the floor where were assembled sets of china, silver services, clocks, kitchen utensils, and stacks of men's hats, guarded by chairs and massive walnut radios.

On one table there were a few books, a stack of records, some sheet music, and a loose assemblage of costume jewelry, including a crucifix or two as well as some crosses on chains. Mr Morse, in trying to be out of the way of the major streams of traffic in which all sorts and sizes of mostly women not without roughness and rudeness worked out their paths through this world's goods, got over near this table and made himself small. He felt a pressure of the bladder crying to be relieved, not seriously as yet, and looked around until he located, across the room, what was evidently a toilet. Not only did he see no specification of gender written near it, however, but its door disconcertingly stood open.

"Should I get this for Mary Elizabeth or do you think it doesn't look new enough?"

A massive red-faced woman in a pink sweater held across her chest a small pink sweater, and another large woman confronting her looked fiercely at the sweater.

"They don't launder well," she said. "They don't go in the machine, you have to do 'em by hand yourself."

The first woman threw the sweater back.

"Maybe some Yardley's lavender bouquet instead," she said.

Idly and nervously, Mr Morse began turning over the books on the table next him: Black Beauty, First Lessons in

Salesmanship, The Book of Common Prayer, Murder on the Moon, Black Beauty, Black Beauty, Tom Swift and His Electric Airship, King Lear, Hamlet, Macbeth, How to Read the Future, 101 Favorite Hymns. . . . His bladder steadily, increasingly, protested.

Don't think about yourself. Think about other things.

"And suppose it's not a drill," said a nearby voice. "Or suppose they're so smart that their intelligence service knows when we have a drill, and that's the time they decide to drop it."

"They won't drop it," said another voice. "They're afraid of what we'd do to them."

Mr Morse impulsively snatched a book up from the table, opened it, and jabbed his finger at a place on the page.

"I was now beginning to grow handsome; my coat had grown fine and soft, and was bright black. I had one white foot and a pretty white star on my forehead. I was thought very handsome; my master would not sell me till I was four years old. . . ."

Mr Morse thought of the old lady in the dress shop, of the children on the playground, of the pyramids of bottles of golden whisky and silver gin. Anxiety was beginning to grab at his collar.

It comes from somewhere and it goes somewhere, he thought darkly, mutteringly, and on the way it makes dreams. It comes up out of the ground, and it makes dreams, and it pisses away into the ground again. He seemed to see a gigantic, cathedral-sized urinal, standing high, porcelain white, towering into the night sky. And the dreams? the electric airships, the murders on the moon, Macbeth, and black, black beauty?

"Everyone may not know what breaking in is, therefore I will describe it. It means to teach a horse to wear a saddle and bridle, and to carry on his back a man, woman, or child; to go just the way they wish, and to go quietly. . . ."

"No signs, Lord, do not send me a sign," moaned Mr Morse.

"This'd be good for Petey," said a woman, "he grows out of things so fast there's no point in getting good."

The basement of the church was filled with intense heat, with the smell of cosmetics and sweat; and every once in a while the baritone voice of that master of these revels came confusedly through the other noises, admonishing people to be calm, assuring them that it would soon be over, suggesting they might find something they needed.

Mr Morse, at the command of nature, struggled across several aisles full of women. In the course of this operation his foot slipped against some object which turned out to be a small bedside radio; this went flying and fell over. Mr Morse resolutely continued his journey.

Arrived by the open door, however, he stood irresolutely by, waiting to see how some more confident person, native to the place, would handle this social situation. But no one approached on this errand. Instead he felt himself taken by the arm and turned firmly about.

"Afraid we really have to hold you responsible for this," said the baritone voice. Mr Morse looked up into the stern yet pleasant face of (evidently) a clergyman, a man having authority.

"Several of these ladies saw it happen," this man persisted. "You kicked this radio." Indeed he was holding up the little radio Mr Morse had stumbled over; its umbilical cord trailed to the floor between them.

"Even if it was an accident," the clergyman said, implying that he was willing to take the broadest view of the matter, "we have found it absolutely necessary to enforce the rule about accidental breakage. We don't want the owner victimized, after all, do we? Fortunately," he permitted a smile to appear, "it won't put you to any great expense. Four-seventy-five, it says here on the back."

Mr Morse, under the pressure of his several anxieties, pointed to his mouth to indicate that he was dumb; pointed to ears and mouth; he became deaf and dumb. In a moment he might become blind if the pressure increased.

"Not a bad little radio," the clergyman was affably saying. "But I'm afraid he doesn't talk English," he added to the ladies who had encircled them. "Radio," he shouted, leaning close to Mr Morse. "You—buy—radio." His mouth elaborately formed the words. "Good—listen—hear things—good." He turned the radio around and pointed so that Mr Morse saw where it said $4.75.

Mr Morse suddenly bolted through the open door of the bathroom and slammed it in all the faces.

It was absolutely dark inside. He felt for the urinal, for a stall, for a toilet bowl. Outside, voices were clamoring confusedly. This room, Mr Morse reflected wildly, was very small even for a bathroom.

At this moment, far overhead, a siren blew the All Clear, and the church bells took it up. The door opened, and there was light.

"I'm afraid that's the broom closet, friend," said the clergyman, and it was apparent he was doing his best to moderate his normally loud voice out of respect for the ladies present, but also to save Mr Morse and himself from embarrassment.

"Let me show you to the—place," he more or less whispered. "Why didn't you say?—oh, of course, I see, I quite see"—as Mr Morse again put his fingers first to his lips, then to his ears.

And taking Mr Morse as though he were a child by the arm, the clergyman led him through the crowds down a long, dimly lit hall to a fine, spacious, cool lavatory. But after this relief the matter of the radio still had to be faced up to, and Mr Morse, unable to argue without abandoning the rôle he had assumed, allowed himself to be interpreted to by gestures and convinced by signs until he drew out his wallet, handed over five dollars, received a quarter in change, accepted the radio with a curt nod of the head as though he perfectly understood, and went up the stairs trailing the radio wire behind him, and so into the sunlight of the same town as before, which no bomb had touched. A small crowd of people stood in front of the church, dazzled by sunlight and having nowhere urgent or special to go.

"A good drill," Mr Morse heard one man saying. "Splendid co-operation. The mayor's committee inspected, and five minutes after the siren there wasn't a soul to be seen."

Mr Morse stopped behind this man.

"It's because we were all dead," he said. "We were all dead in the buildings, which had all fallen in, like the temple of Dagon. But there were no corpses in the streets, so the mayor will be pleased."

He walked away with his radio, hearing the surprised chuckles behind him, and one man calling after him, "Play up and play the game, buster, just like the rest of us."

Mr Morse continued to walk away. He wondered if the radio would work, and decided that he did not much care one way or the other, for if it worked that would be a sign, and if it didn't work that would be a sign, too.

The Native in the World

THE CLIMB from sleep was difficult, a struggle up a staircase of soft pillows into which he sank again and again, drowsily defeated, from which he clumsily climbed again to a sight of the room that, seen in the equivocal wisdom of sleep, seemed to him any room, or all the rooms, in which he had ever slept, or ever been at home. Perhaps (an instant afterward he could no longer remember)—perhaps the phrase 'at home' struck the first tone of clarity in his mind, for about it the room began to arrange itself, to become again the familiar fashion of his circumstance, rising and composing to his own composition of its features. One thing—the overturned chair by the desk, with his clothes crushed under it—remained obstinately unfamiliar; when had he done that? He searched his memory, but the incident had sunk under sleep; he could readily imagine himself coming in drunk and knocking the chair down in the effort to hang his clothes over it, but actually to remember doing it—that was a different thing.

He got out of bed, and as he stood up felt pain protest harshly in his forehead, making him dizzy with the angry sleep that would not readily dissolve. The clock said ten more or less exactly and it was dark outside. That meant twenty hours sleep; since two Tuesday morning. The dizziness surged higher as he bent in a methodical stupor to set the chair right and get his clothes. Going into the next room he started the phonograph and put on the Ricercare of the Musikalische Opfer; then settled back in the darkness of a far corner. The one voice strode through his mind with a more or less plaintive confidence that another would follow, and soon another did, then one more and another, and the rest were sunken in the ensemble and the scratch of the needle. He closed his eyes, and as if his consciousness rested on quicksand he was irresistibly sucked back toward sleep, his eyelids grew heavy in a sort of undertow that he could feel heavily about his head. A dream, some frightening and fast forgotten dream, jarred him out of sleep; he had a vague impression of fear, something was being thrown at him. He turned on the light, changed over the record and picked up a book that was lying on the couch: *Alcohol the Friend of Man*. It was a reassuring volume by a doctor of unspecified repute; one must, he thought, turning over the pages, combine theory with practice. It seemed to him, as he had so often said, that there was a way to drink seriously, and a way not to drink seriously. Of three years at Harvard he had spent the last two learning the former, and was glad to distinguish himself from many of his acquaintances whose drinking was of the rowdy-up-and-puke sort. If a man wish to drink himself into insensibility, he phrased it pedantically, that is his own business; but equally he should not become a charge on his fellow-beings, and there is no excuse for forgetting manners one instant before passing out.

The record was over, and he walked across the room to change it, a strange figure in white pajamas, barefoot, head slightly too large for his excessively small frail body. He already had on his silver-rimmed reading glasses; he must have picked them up from the desk without thinking. He came from the Middle West, but one would unhesitatingly have called him a Yankee, judging by his pedantic contemptuous manner, his manners so civil as to be rude whenever he gave a cutting edge to his voice. His own estimate of himself was quite accurate: that his aloofness was respected, also his enormous and casual erudition; that even full professors were chary of a too great freedom with him or with his papers; that it was generally said of him that he would go far if he did not drink himself to death; that his paper on Augustinianism in the 17th century would no doubt put him in line for a fellowship; and at last, that he was drinking himself to death,

or near to it—a state which he conceived of dubiously as a
slight chill in his personal weather, as though a cloud should
slide over a hill on which he was sunning himself. As to his
reasons—if a man wish to drink himself into insensibility, he
thought again . . . and perhaps it is not even his own business,
or perhaps it is a shady transaction in that business, into which
he does well not to inquire too far; look what happened to
Oedipus.

He had put on the Ricercare again, but now he turned it off
in the middle and called Rico's number. He listened apprehen-
sively to the empty buzz of the phone, three, four, five times:
he could hear it as if he were in the room, but as if the room
were still empty, the lonely stupid ringing. Damn Rico, he
thought, damn the twisted little Cuban Jesuit gone wrong,
and damn, he said, and damn with the ring of the phone, and
damn again and hung up. The receiver clattered into its
cradle, and he felt again how painfully slow it was to wake
up, how fiercely he must fight to stay above the surface, so to
speak, to force every last ache and hurt in body and mind to
the service of wakefulness, to a nagging insistence on belief in
being awake. Rico was probably out with Alan; Alan, he
thought angrily, the little blond jew-boy who's trying to get
me out of the way by advising me seriously to go see a
psychiatrist. And Rico is helping him too.

He shuddered slightly, envisioning conspiracy and betrayal: the swift, sure honest-eyed kiss of treachery, the bright,
the clear, the trustworthy Judas; and the appalling thing was
that it took place on such a pitifully small scale, the love life of
a colony of worms. The disgust, and the hate, were waking
him, slowly, as one fever will fight another and overcome it.

He took up the phone again and called Rhys. One could
always talk to Rhys, no matter how far they had gone apart.
Long ago, before the drinking, as he thought, they had been
close friends, working furiously together, reading two and

three books in an evening and listening to Bach from two to four in the morning. And then—there had been no break, not even a coolness; but they went their ways and saw rather less of each other. When he was drunk and wanted to talk out of turn, he often still climbed to Rhys' room, and he would talk wildly for fifteen minutes, often incoherently, and then Rhys would deliberate heavily, and say at last, "Well, John, it's difficult . . ." which in itself would be somewhat reassuring; and then they would exhaust a small stock of polite and cynically erudite remarks about obscure poets, or faculty members, and it would be over.

"Hello, Rhys? This is John—Bradshaw. . . . I hope I didn't disturb you?"

"Not at all," said Rhys, in the coldly amiable tones that meant he was disturbed.

"Look, Rhys, . . . you mustn't mind me; I'm not drunk, but I took twelve grains of amytal last night when I was. I've just managed to get out of bed and I'm a little—woozy." He was, in fact, woozier than he had thought; there was that dull weight on his forehead that was worse than pain, more unknown and more fearful therefore.

"What I wanted to know was could you meet me for a drink, about fifteen minutes from now?"

"No, I can't," said Rhys. "You sound troubled. I don't know medicine, but isn't twelve grains rather much?"

"The prescribed adult dose is a grain and a half. I wish you'd come out for a drink. I want to talk to you. Really, you know, it gets to be too much, sometimes . . . everywhere you go people are such bitches. . . ."

"What the hell is wrong, John?"

"Oh,—look, I'm liable to ramble a bit—I'm not very awake and the drug is still pretty strong—Oh goddam it Rhys, I've been betrayed, I—"

"Again?" A politely skeptical coolness.

Steady, he thought to himself; he was weak and falling again, and before answering he bit his lower lip hard, till the blood ran, to save himself from sleep.

"I mean it," he said stubbornly.

"Yes," said Rhys; and John recognized the tone Rhys used to nice drunks. "Yes, people are . . . difficult sometimes."

"Rhys, I'm not drunk. I want to talk to you. Why won't you have a drink with me?"

"Because I don't feel like it, John."

"Rhys, you think I'm drunk. I'm not, Rhys. It's the amytal. I couldn't be drunk, Rhys, I just got up, I've slept since two this morning."

"I know you're not drunk, John," said Rhys coldly. "I'm busy, and I think you ought to go back to bed. You don't sound very well."

"I only want to talk to you about Rico. You think I'm drunk."

"What's Rico done now?"

"I want to talk to you, Rhys."

"Well . . .?"

"Not on the phone."

"All right then, good night."

"Rhys—"

"Good night."

He waited for the dead click at the other end, and then placed the receiver carefully down. That had been a shameful performance; he was not drunk, but he could not have been more maudlin in any case. Rhys would be nodding his head sagely at this very moment: poor John Bradshaw. Oh, damn Rhys. It was unfair of him. He might have had the common courtesy to listen to me, Rhys the careful, Rhys the undrunk, the dullard so proud of his dullness; one could summon up at will that favorite image of Rhys the damned, sitting deep in his armchair after a peculiarly bitter confessional period, sitting like a tolerant father-confessor, saying slowly between puffs at a cigarette, "Gawd, all you people live such exciting lives—it must be so difficult for you—you come and tell me about drinking and drugs and your homosexual experiences— and I sit here on my can, taking it all in, living my dull life . . . ." And he would sit there on his can, looking as old as he could, and staring into the fire, saying "they also serve," or some such. Poor Rhys! And so anxious, too, for you to know that he was only pretending dullness (which God knows he was not) and that he was a man of deep spiritual crises; as he would say, and so smugly, "My blowups all take place in- side." All right. Let Rhys take that attitude. He wasn't required.

He got to his feet and walked slowly about the room, still thinking about Rhys, beating one little fist determinedly into the other hand and thinking with melancholy savagery, "cut away the non-essentials, cut them out." Rhys was a non- essential, Rhys always worrying about his writing, his pid- dling poetry, his painful anxiety that you read his newest work, that you pat him on the head, that you say nice things. . . . As for himself, he thought, there would be a book one day . . . a book after this long silence, after the non-essentials had been cut away and meditation had burned some great stone to form inside him, a book that would say all these things that had to be said, against the lying time, against the lying treacherous people, against Rhys, against Rico, against Alan, against (he sneered) all these smilers with their dull knives. One voice in his wilderness would not waste time crying out for help, for cries would only bring the wolves along faster. And through this, beneath the pain and the hate and the disgust and still half-prevailing sleep, he knew that he was crying out.

He went into the bathroom and looked at the bottle of amytal. There were at least twenty-five grains left; he smiled a little to remember the time when one grain could give him a solid night's sleep, the rapid necessity to step up the dose, the doctor at the hygiene building telling him pedagogically that he was by definition a drug-addict, his crazily epigrammatic crypticism to the doctor ("Jonathan Swift was by definition not a well man, and a neurotic to boot"), his cheerful announcement to Rhys (Rhys again): "You may call me De Quincey, I'm depraved." It was the precipitous, the plunging rapidity with which it had happened, this drug business, that astounded him and started slight inadmissible fears from their careful rest. How one thing led to another! in such seemingly inconsequential succession of one pettiness on the next, until, looking back from the most extravagantly fantastic heights of improbability, from the most unwarranted excesses and distortions, one was surprised and shocked to note how accurately and how unerringly every smallest act, word and gesture quietly conspired to build such a wildly rococo and out-of-the-way edifice,—such a goblin's architecture that at one moment one shuddered to think how it drove one on to the end, and at the next dismissed the whole structure with a smile for its implausibility. He stared fixedly at the bottle, imagined himself reaching out for it, tried to imagine himself refusing, and could only get a more or less chromo reproduction of a man in a magazine advertisement with his head turned disaffectedly away from a cup of coffee, saying: "Nope, I keep away from it. Keeps me up nights." This did not seem to him a satisfactory image of moral grandeur; with a smile he took up the bottle and locked it away in the filing cabinet on his desk. Then, puzzled, he looked at the key to the cabinet; what to do with that? He took it with him into the living room. He stood in the very center of the carpet, shut his eyes and turned around thrice, as though he were absurdly playing some children's game of blind man's buff; with his eyes still tightly closed, he threw the key straight before him, heard it tinkle in landing, then turned around twice more before opening his eyes. A glance about the room satisfied him that the key was not in evidence, not obviously anyhow. It might be days before he came across it. Unless the chamber-maid picked it up in the morning. He could imagine that she might hand it to him, asking whether he had lost it, and imagine himself saying no, I wonder how it could have got here . . . but one couldn't do that; all one's correspondence was in the filing cabinet, and notes for a couple of essays as well. Anyhow, it would be easy to find the key again, when it was really required. Meanwhile, one could . . . imagine it lost.

He decided to give Rico one more chance, and dialled his number again. The equivocal ringing—does it ring if you're not there to hear it?—angered him; he thought it possible that Rico and Alan were in the room, refusing to answer, he could hear them guessing who it might be, smiling complacently, drifting from smiles into their moonings and caressings, their adolescent, ill-informed lecheries—but no, neither one of them would have the strength to let the phone ring and keep on ringing; across each ugly infirm purpose would flash thoughts of importance, of some great person, some missed opportunity, the thought especially: it might be something better. And they would answer the phone. Rico particularly would answer the phone, compliant opportunist, affection's whore . . . had he ever done differently, or been anything else? Rico? who told (with pride) how he had been seduced by the house-maid when he was fifteen, and how three weeks later he had gone to his mother and got the girl discharged on some pretext.

No, they would answer the phone, he knew, and since they had not . . . Perhaps they weren't even together; he cut the call short and dialled Alan's room. Alan's roommate answered:

"Hello."

"Hello, is Alan there?"

"No, he went out half an hour ago."

"Was Rico with him?"

"I think he was going to meet Rico. Is there any message I can give him?"

"No thanks."

"Your name . . .?"

"No thanks," he said coldly and replaced the receiver. He thought desperately for a moment that he might call Rhys again, then rejected the idea. There was no sense in begging. He felt tired again; the weight in his forehead had turned into a headache, and his eyes tended to water. The slight exertion of walking about the room made him want to go to bed, but he refused, and to clinch his refusal, began to get dressed. A drink was probably what was needed, he thought. A drink, and an hour out of this room. There was the mood he had been in all too often lately: his room depressed him, almost as much as did a library, for example; and the best things in the room,—the Matisse over the victrola, for example—they were so recognized, so much the very breath of this tepid climate that they became unbearable, and music was unbearable, and work as well, and it all seemed to him the ugly and ready-to-hand diversion afforded a man sentenced to life imprisonment. Not the ugly, but the commonplace disgusts, he thought. If they put Matisses in the street-cars, one would counter by hanging advertisements on one's walls. Yet he felt unsatisfied outside his room, again like a prisoner so acclimated as to shun freedom; a walk, however short, tired him inordinately, and climbing two flights to the room made his head throb as if the blood would burst out. He felt now that he required a drink; he would go to St. Clair's, nor did he disguise from himself the fact that half his motive was to find Rico, and that if Rico were not at St. Clair's he might be at Bella Vista, or McBride's, or the Stag Club, or he might be in town at the Napoleon or the Ritz or the Lincolnshire.

By the time he had finished dressing he found himself nearly exhausted. He had to sit down on the couch and turn out the light, and it was then that he began to think about the key to the filing-cabinet. He felt that he had perhaps been foolish, with his infantile stratagem. He might need the key in a hurry, for his notes, or to answer a letter, or—no need to disguise the fact from himself—to get the amytal when he came in drunk; it had to be conveniently to hand, or he would get no sleep. He must recognize the fact by now, he argued: he required the amytal, he was a mature individual, still sane, heaven knows, more sane than most of his dull acquaintances, he would not over-dose. And anyhow, the test was in the will to stay off the stuff, not in locking it away, there was no help in that. To be able to keep it before his eyes, that bottle, to look at it steadily, and steadfastly not to take it—at least not more than was absolutely necessary—there was the thing. Besides, suppose he needed it in a hurry, sometime, and the key had got lost—there were any number of ways that could have happened: it might have fallen into a crack in the floor, might have slid under the carpet, might even have landed down the radiator gratings, irretrievable short of large-scale operations that would require the janitor.

Hastily he turned on the light, began to look around. It was not that he wanted any now, or would take any tonight; but this was the saner thing to do, he must know.

The key was discovered with ridiculous ease, under the bookcase. He picked it up and laid it carefully in the middle drawer of his desk. And unformed to speech or even to clear thought, but present in his mind, was that justification, that ritual against reason, of a postulated higher power, of unspecified nature, watching over the episode, the feeling, carefully swathed in obscurity: Providence didn't want me to hide the key, or I wouldn't have found it so easily.

Put vaguely at ease, he began to get on his overcoat, and then decided to call Rhys again, buoyed up by this same vague assurance that he would, by however narrow a margin, do the thing which was to be done, that the thing would be right because he did it. But there was no answer, and for some reason, he was more infuriated at this than at Rico's absence—a little relieved, too, for Rhys would have been annoyed; but angry, angry that Rhys should not be there, should have gone out after making some excuse to him. Betrayal, he thought, furiously and without power. Rhys too. Although loneliness was his habitual way, it was by preference, because it suited him to be alone, but this, the loneliness by compulsion, was a new thing. He felt a terrible isolation, the phone seemed to him now only an instrument of the Inquisition, to teach him his loneliness as it were by rote, and he had the sudden sense that whatever number he called, it would be closed to him by that instrument. In fact, he thought in satiric anger—in fact this whole room is given only to people who want to be left alone. It is made to teach them the measure—that is, the unmeasurable quality—of isolation, of being absolutely alone. Harvard College built it that way—they get a lot of lonely ones around here.

The brief walk in the cold, up Dunster street and across the Square to St. Clair's, fatigued him excessively; he recognized that last night's dose had not nearly worn off, and that the cold had the unusual effect of making him want to lie down and go to sleep just wherever he was, in the street even. It was almost like being drunk, that disgusting soddenness with drink that made it Nirvana just to stop moving, anyhow, anywhere. He kept up his heart to a degree by repeating his little catechism of betrayal, his interdict on Rico and on Rhys, all the fictions of his misery forming into churches for his martyred self: here was a first station, where one knelt to beg forgiveness for being rude to Bradshaw; and here a second, where one knelt to do penance for being out when Bradshaw called, here another for thinking Bradshaw drunk when he wasn't, here another for the general sin of offending Bradshaw; and a last, where one prayed for the grace of Bradshaw: Oh Bradshaw, we do beseech thee . . . and a return for the petty humiliations, and a hundred-fold paid back each error, and he knew it for pitiful, but nevertheless went on, in a rage of cynical benevolence, to forgive Rico, to forgive Rhys, to forgive them and cut them away from his side, and to go on in the thorough lonely discretion of his anger.

When he entered St. Clair's the first person he saw was Rhys, big, rather stout, and darkly dressed as usual, sitting by himself at a corner table. Rhys waved and beckoned to the chair opposite, and John sat down there.

"You're avoiding me," he said without thinking; his anger came to a head and he wanted a fight.

"If I were avoiding you, would I come and sit in a bar?" asked Rhys politely, and it was like being hit across the face.

"Then why did you tell me you couldn't go out?"

"I didn't say I couldn't go out. I said I didn't feel like going out." Rhys was nettled, and showed it by getting more and more polite.

"If you don't want to see me, I won't sit here."

"Don't be silly. Sit around and have a drink."

Rhys, he thought, was playing for a dull peace and it was not to be allowed; he must be disturbed, made to give himself away. He ordered, and got, a large martini, and sipped it in an uneasy silence.

"You should have gone to bed. You look as if you were trying to kill yourself." Rhys gave in and said something.

"What the hell would you care?" he asked rhetorically, hoping at the same time that Rhys would say something friendly and reassuring.

"How is it possible for anyone to care? You're not very responsive to care, you know."

"Oh, some have managed." He lit a cigarette. It tasted very

bad, but it was against the sleep that even the drink seemed to drive him at. The place where he had bit his lip was still tender, it hurt when he spoke.

"You alienate even those," said Rhys. It was for him as though he had said 'where are you, John?' and reached out a hand in the darkness; it was such an unwelcome thing to be forced to find people when ordinarily they came and disclosed themselves.

They finished their drinks in silence and ordered more.

"Now what's this about Rico?" said Rhys at last.

John emptied his glass again, slowly, before answering. "It's only that from now on," he said, "I'm going to play dirty too. If you don't what chance have you got?"

"I always thought of Rico as more or less irresponsible," said Rhys, "but—"

"It's not only Rico, God knows. He can be excused: if you were bounced out of a parochial school in Cuba and landed at Harvard with the prospect of eight million bucks when you came out—alors. Not alone Rico, no. It's everyone. And you too, sir. Don't you understand: I'm playing your way now, the safe way you all play, don't give anything with one hand that you can't get back with both, any time. And if I can't beat these Jesuits at their own game—well, what the hell . . ." he shrugged his thin shoulders, deliberately blew smoke across the table between them.

Rhys determined to show no annoyance, to maintain objectivity. So he sat with hands out equally on the table, looking like the balance-pans of the blind goddess.

"Essentially stupid attitude to take," he said. "I mean—granting that people do present . . . difficulties at times—still, just how much have you got hurt?"

"Got hurt, hell. That's not—"

"You don't need to answer me," continued Rhys with a show of calm. "I'm just suggesting the question as something for you to worry about."

"Don't go on; you had it right the first time, when you said something about responsibility. You just make an ass of yourself when you put it on the piddling level of 'getting hurt.' It's only a question of how the essential non-pirate is to live in a world of pirates."

Rhys had no immediate reply to this, so they ordered more drinks and John continued:

"Romans and Orthodox Jews make the best pirates because even if they do put pretty far out to sea after plunder, they've both got a sailor's snug harbor to get to again. The Catholic can drop anchor in a church, the Jew carries his absolution along on shipboard. But they aren't the only ones, not by a long shot. It applies to everyone you know . . . piracy isn't so safe a game for them, but if you think for a minute—"

"I wish you wouldn't pretend to sit in judgment when you're looking so pitifully ill. You remind me not so much of the Christian Way as of Nietzsche."

And suddenly John felt the fatigue again, the wish to give it up; what was the use in arguing with Rhys. The drink was having an inordinate effect because of the amytal. He knew it would be difficult to get up, next to impossible to walk home.

"Hell," he said. "It's only an argument for you. Forget the whole thing." And then: "Will you take me home?"

"What's wrong? Not feeling well?"

"I'm sick to death of sitting here with you, listening to your well-fed brain. I want to leave and I can't do it by my-self. I'm asking you: as one last favor, would you see me home? Let me assure you, sir, it will be the last. I shan't disturb you and your values again."

"Please don't be melodramatic with me, John," said Rhys in a quiet rage.

"Can't you see that's not the question?"

"Don't you think you'd feel better if you sat here without drinking for a few minutes?"

"Oh for heaven's sake, sir, don't be reasonable with me. I've asked you a question, will you—"

He felt a draught on his back from the open door. Shivering extravagantly, with the hope that Rhys would think him ill, he turned and saw Rico and Alan standing beside his chair.

"Wha's wrong, little one," asked Rico, slightly drunk, smiling with his beautiful teeth.

"Rico!" He held out his hand, forgetting Rhys, forgetting Alan. "Rico"—and more softly, as though drawing the other into conspiracy—"will you take me home? I can't go myself."

"Sure, little one. I can take you home. Come, give me your hand." Rico laughed, his laugh and his glance taking in the whole room, stranger and intimate alike, as though to disclaim all embarrassment and responsibility, as though to enlist their sympathy not for John but for self-sacrificing Rico who had to take him home.

"Come," he said. "Up on your feet."

He got to his feet slowly enough, his eyes half fading from their focus. The floor seemed to rock beneath him, his ears filled with noise, and it was as if he stood on a separate planet that rocked backwards and over in space, out of sight of Rhys who sat there with an embarrassed expression on his face. Then suddenly he knew he was heavily in Rico's arms, and in one instant synapse of sobriety he heard himself saying to Rhys, "I hate you more..." and Rico saying roughly, "Come on," pulling at his arm. Then the two little voices were again swept away in a wave of sound against his brain, formless sound at first, that resolved itself into a rhythm and at length into words spoken from far away: "Drink and drugs that done him in," or some such; and then—drink and drugs—he could no longer hear for noise, but the enormous voice of Rico was in his head saying "Come on, come on," and all at once they were in the street and the cold stung his eyes and the sweat on his cheeks.

Rico and Alan had taken him by the arms, close to the

shoulder, and were dragging him along. Whenever he stumbled they set him right with a jerk that lifted his feet off the ground.

"Wait," he said. "Sick."

And while they stood silently by holding him, Rico holding his head forward, he was sick, with a horrible violence, in a little alley off Dunster street. His stomach, almost empty to start with, twisted painfully at the finish, and he lost consciousness.

When he came to he was alone in his room with Rico. He could not see Alan anywhere. He rested on his bed and Rico was taking his clothes off. There was no longer any rest, or desire to sleep; there was only pain in his stomach and an actively hurtful weariness.

Rico finished stripping him, folded him in between the sheets. "You'll be OK in the morning," he said. "You were sick as a bitch. How d'you feel now?"

"Rico," he whispered. "Don't go away, Rico." He felt distantly that he was a child, in his child's bed at home; he had done a wrong thing, and Rico would be angry, with the efficient necessary anger of a mother.

"Kiss me, Rico," he said. "Kiss me good night." And then, as Rico made no move to comply, he said: "You're mad at me . . .?" with a pathetic dubious note of shame in his voice, and Rico stooped and quickly kissed him on the cheek.

"Now good night, little one."

"Don't go, Rico. Stay here tonight."

"I can't. You'll be all right now."

"But I won't, Rico. I won't. I'll be sick again." He grew panicky with new fear. "I swear I'll be sick again," he said. "The minute you leave. Don't leave, Rico."

Then, in a tone of malicious invalid craft, he said accusingly: "You gave Alan the key to your room, didn't you?" Breathless, he went on: "You told him to wait in your room, didn't you."

Rico's face gave him away; it was true, it could only be true. "That's why you want to leave," he went on. "I know why." Quietly he began to whimper, and the tears rolled down his face. Then in a desperate martyrdom he said in a choked voice: "I'll kill myself if you go. I'll kill myself the minute you go out that door."

"Nonsense, what would you do it with, little one." Rico was not very good at situations like this; he felt vaguely that he should comfort, should sacrifice himself a little and help; but he had no intelligent means of doing it, being frightened not by a lie, but by a lie that would involve him later.

"I'd take all the amytal. I would. It would be enough. You'd see it would be enough. Rico, don't be a bastard. Don't go away."

"You mustn't do that, John. You mustn't think of it."

"And you can't find the amytal either. I hid it." There was a terrible cunning in his voice, he was determined to have the drug. It did not at that time matter to him whether it was a lethal dose or not; it was to spite Rico, to hurt him, to say to him: 'See what might have happened. The guilt would have been yours, you would have murdered me.'

Rico went to the bathroom to look for the amytal.

"You can't find it, you can't," he mocked in a thin voice cracked with approaching hysteria. "Go away, damn you. Go away."

Rico came back into the room.

"You won't do it, John."

"Get out."

"Promise me you won't do it."

"Get out."

"If you don't promise I can't do anything."

"I said get out."

Rico was faced with something beyond his comprehension, and he took the only way he understood.

"All right," he said sullenly. "I guess it's your life." And having thus washed himself clean in his own eyes, he walked out.

There was no question of decision, now he was alone. It was again that unfaced trust in a higher power, in some back world watching. With unnecessary stealth he got out of bed and, entirely naked, went to the desk, got the key and opened the filing cabinet. He took the bottle into the bathroom and poured all the pills into a highball glass, which he filled with warm water. This decoction he took back into the living room, where he sat down on the couch by the phone and began to drink. When the glass was empty there remained a considerable residue of damp powder at the bottom, so he refilled the glass and started again, more slowly, from time to time stirring the mixture with a pencil. At last he had finished. From experience, he knew there would be about fifteen minutes to wait.

He turned on all the lights, not feeling like getting into bed again. As he stood naked in the corner by the light-switch he was taken suddenly with a frenzy. The thing was done, it was done. Was it right? was it so at all? The indecision after the event frightened him, he imagined the maid finding him in the morning and with a certain sense of abject shame rushed to put his bathrobe about him. How to know? He questioned if he should be saved, and then, as he became somewhat more calm, there occurred to him another of those tests of providence, another cryptic question to which the oracle might smilingly equivocate over his special case.

He took up the phone and dialled Rhys' number. If Rhys answered he would explain and have him get a doctor. If there were no answer . . . and as he listened to the ring he felt certain there must be. It was not so much the test of fate, but the thought that he must speak again to Rhys, apologize, absolve, ask forgiveness.

There was no answer. Unwilling to believe, he put the

phone down on the table and let it ring. The answer was given, but unsatisfactorily only more or less given, with the smiling ambiguity of power. He went to the window and opened it, then sat back on the couch. It is doubtful that he thought any more of death, of the probability or the certainty. He listened to the dried icy branches of the trees scratch together in the wind, down in the courtyard; and it is doubtful that he thought of leaving anything behind, of regret, or the irrevocability of death.

For his room, warm with the lights full on, seemed to him some tall citadel of the sun, with a certain congenial ease of sunlight upon it, and when the sleep came down, it drifted in like the cool sudden shadow of a cloud, that only made him shudder slightly.

The Idea of a University

ON SUNDAY MORNINGS President Ramshorn inspected his university, or at least went around it with one of his deans, this morning Dean Bildad of the Graduate School of Divinity. The president chose Sunday for this tour because almost no one was about, and there would be relatively little bowing and scraping to acknowledge.

Because it was the first Sunday of term, and maybe because of the presence of Dean Bildad, the occasion lent itself to wistful philosophizing on the themes of grandeur, achievement, and the passing away of men and worlds. The president began.

"What talent I've got," he said, "is for money. Don't think I don't realize that's why I'm here. Look at that now, Bill."

"That," still mostly hidden by foliage, was the new Aero Engineering Building, a long glass-and-metal shed slanting from the middle of the Park into the space between two old red-brick buildings given to the mellower studies of English and History.

"There didn't seem anywhere else to put it," said the president. "And even then they had to take down the Trysting Elm to get one of those fighters through the doors. But you've got to move ahead, you can't stand still."

"Place has changed," Dean Bildad said, "since we were undergraduates. World much harder to see around nowadays. Did you know that the kids can major in Hairdressing now? in Cosmetic Chemistry? in Fashion Design?"

"It was the Angel Azazel," President Ramshorn reminded him, "who taught men the art of war and women how to paint their faces. Book of Enoch. And of course I know everything that goes on here."

"Apocryphal," said Bildad, and the two men walked on in silence until he took up the theme again. "I've just remembered that when I studied Physics you weighed things with spring balances. A spring balance, now, is something I can understand. A touching little instrument, with a homey charm all its own. I don't imagine they'd let a spring balance through the back door these days."

"No, they have somewhat more, ah, sophisticated methods now," the president vaguely allowed. "When I spoke of knowing everything, a moment back, I meant, of course, in a general way and with respect to its administration. Even Solomon, dear Bill, though quite correct in choosing wisdom, didn't know everything, but only everything pertaining to earthly rule."

"The world is too specialized," Dean Bildad agreed, if it was agreement. "No one—or so I'm told—can even know his own field any more."

"I certainly hope that isn't true," the president replied, "especially considering the salaries we pay some of these fellows nobody can quite say what they're about. What is slow light, Bill, would you know?"

Dean Bildad said it might maybe refer to the dawn of understanding in a student's head.

"I don't have to know exactly," the president went on, "but I would like to know if it means something just a shade off the standard figure—these scientists make their triumphs on what seems so little sometimes—or whether the stuff really does just creep across the floor. We've bought this fellow name of Mordecai Bosch, got him in out of Austria; well, he received the Nobel Prize for 'the invention of slow light,' that's what the citation said in the *Times*. Those Swedes must have had expert opinion; he's got to know what he's about—but how would you check? He doesn't teach, of course, he just thinks."

"You could ask him."

"Oh, I wouldn't want to do that," the president said;

obviously he had already rejected this solution. "He's a very tetchy fellow, his English isn't good . . . They've had some trouble with him already, you see, because he hasn't got clearance. The Security Officer tried to explain to him, and did explain to his colleagues, that the Project wasn't to be mentioned in his presence till his clearance came through. So he sulked, Bosch did, for several days, and then began coming around during coffee breaks and committing breaches of security; it seems he thinks classified thoughts."

"What project would that be, now?"

"Well, Bill, I'm not allowed to say. But Defense thinks a great deal of it, I can tell you that."

Having completed their tour of the Park and its circumjacent buildings, they now boarded the president's limousine for a survey of the outlying precincts. Whitman, the Negro chauffeur, held open the door for them, and then resumed his place at the wheel.

"It's not only specialization," the president said, referring back a bit, "but integration."

Dean Bildad placed a finger before his lips, then indicated with it the Negro's back.

"Integration of disciplines," President Ramshorn went on, "confusion of fields. Fifty years back, Bill, a chemist stayed in one building and a physicist stayed in another building. Chemistry was cooking and Physics was playing with blocks. Atoms were bricks and there was no nonsense about three dozen invisible pieces inside them. Economists had never heard of anthropologists—no more had theologians—see what I mean? The world was more dignified, as well as simpler.

"I tell you, Bill," he went on, "a young fellow Clemence, in Math, at dinner the other night—Grace and I have them to dinner, you know—he was trying to explain to me what a Lobachevskian triangle would look like, and why; well, I tell you, I was morally affronted. Not because he drew it on the tablecloth, no, but because a triangle has got to add up to a hundred and eighty degrees, or the world is going to hell!" He slapped the seat beside him in emphasis, and added: "A razor made of glue!"

"What?"

"Time. He said that time was a razor made of glue. Brr." The dean nodded.

"What you say is true in my bailiwick too, Fred. We've got a good school, I think, and in one way you might figure Christianity has never been more popular, especially with the intellectuals. But sometimes I wonder if it's Christianity. In our day a kid went to Divinity to be ordained, and go out to preach—theology, criticism, homiletics, Hebrew and Greek, that's what he studied. Then Comparative Religion got big. The utter silliness of a curriculum," he suddenly exploded, "that puts that sort of thing in a Divinity School just because it has 'religion' in the title. If I had my way, Comp. Rel. would either be got rid of entirely or be taught as far as possible from our lot—on the Agricultural campus, maybe."

"You can't go back into the past, I guess," said the president.

The Car was rolling through a rundown neighborhood of sagging frame houses bordering the railroad; Negro families were sunning themselves on the steps.

"Sooner or later," said the dean, "we'll have to buy up all this and clean it out. The town won't do it, and we need the land. The way it is now, our buildings are all dispersed over the landscape and the town pushes in between."

"This here?" President Ramshorn was surprised. "This does belong to the university," he explained. "It's our model slum."

"Is that—is it, well, ethical?" the dean inquired after a long pause.

"It's a very big project," answered the president. "Sociology wanted it badly, Economics wanted it for some studies they were doing, the Political Scientists found they could use it to good effect on local government, then the Anthropologists got in the act . . . Finally everybody could see it as one huge integrated project, the Lasswell Foundation put up matching funds, we got the Department of Fine Arts to use faculty architects—and we went right ahead. Imported the tenants from Georgia. I assure you, Bill," he added earnestly, "it's an improvement in their situation, a real improvement. And of course it makes a situation where they can be studied. They've got their own churches, of course, if that's what you meant."

The car stopped beside an enclave of buildings new and old, large and small.

"Psychometrics," the president said. "I believe they study children."

"They are in my business too," the Dean assured him. "They are trying to induce religious ecstasy in a selected group of divinity students and make electroencephalographs of the results; they say they are correlating Unitive Experience with variation of the Alpha rhythm."

"You don't say," said the president, and both men got out of the car.

Approaching the entrance of a white marble building without windows, the two men were stopped by a sentry, one of two armed MPS who flanked the iron door.

"Sorry," he said. "Authorized Personnel only. I'll have to see your passes."

"Young man," said Dr Ramshorn, "I am the president of this university."

"Can't anything be done about that, sir," the young man replied civilly enough.

"We didn't actually want to go in," said the president, "only to walk around."

"Not allowed," said the sentry.

"Young man," Dr Ramshorn said, "I'll take your name and serial number, and I can promise you are going to hear about this; if necessary the Base Commander is going to hear about it. This is my university."

On hearing this the sentry presented arms, making an effect of deference and defense together.

"I wouldn't push it, Fred," advised Dean Bildad in a whisper. But now the president smiled.

"Good man, soldier," he said. "Strict obedience, letter of the law, no exceptions. Just testing," he added, "just testing."

Taking Dean Bildad by the arm, President Ramshorn, evidently pleased, turned him gently back toward the car.

"I bet we're the only campus in the country," he said, "with a Maximum Security Experimental Prison."

"An oddly elegant though appropriately tomblike arrangement," said Dean Bildad.

"It was built for the Art people," said the president, "to house the Caithness Collection. Then the Caithness Collection was torpedoed on the way over, but luckily the courts held that we had already accepted it formally and were paying the freight in an American bottom, so the insurance went to us. That's how we built the new all-denominational chapel," he added, "so you can see how everything adds up in the end."

"What do they do in there?" asked the dean, taking a glance back at the prison.

"Defense is doing studies in brain-washing, Bill. The Korea business got them mighty scared. They don't call it brainwashing, of course. I bet you couldn't guess the code name for the operation?"

"I guess I couldn't," said the dean.

"Operation Dry Clean," said the president, grinning, "because American brains couldn't stand the shrinkage, get it?"

"I get it."

"General Maclehose told me that. Got a keen sense of fun, General Maclehose."

Whitman held the door open, and the two got back in the limousine. Off they went toward the completion of their rounds.

"I like making this tour," said President Ramshorn. "Oh, I know we don't actually *do* much, but it kind of reassures me that everything is in its right place. And I get to know you fellows better, too. After all," he added with much seriousness, "a university gets its name because it is modeled on the universe. Whatever they have out there, we have here too."

But now it neared noon, and activity increased in and around the campus. For the last item on their tour, the president had Whitman halt the car briefly before the plate-glass front of their newest installation, the Random Access Computer Unit. Inside the window were visible several metal boxes, a couple of consoles, and a large typewriter which, with no evidence of human control or for that matter attention, was patiently printing something across and down an apparently endless roll of paper that fed in turn into a large but overflowing wastebasket.

The Nature of the Task

PALEN'S FIRST ASSIGNMENT seemed a simple one, though somewhat demeaning: he was supposed to kill the flies in the room. Not his own room, the one he slept in and to which he was returned at intervals for the other necessities of life, but another room, one which had the appearance of being specially devised, Palen could not quite say for what—not merely as a place in which flies were killed, certainly; but it just had that intentional look, austere and technical. For one thing, it was square, as near as he could tell an exact cube, and unfurnished but for one window, also square and set so high in a corner that nothing could be seen but sky and the tip of a single tree without leaves. The window was divided by iron bars into a lattice of nine equal squares, and by a screen of fine, black mesh beyond the bars, so that the sky, the single tree, the passing cloud, even the occasional bird, appeared superimposed on a graph.

No fly was either visible or audible at first—which was not to say, Palen reminded himself, that there were no flies in the room. For the speckled linoleum of the floor, the pitted acoustical tiles of the ceiling, and the wallpaper, patterned of dark-blue snowflakes ceaselessly failing to fall, offered, probably by design, an ideal camouflage for a quiescent fly—he remembered that flies were said never to sleep, but they sometimes sat still, he was fairly sure of that—who might at any moment reveal himself.

Palen could not help acknowledging a feeling of chagrin about the humble nature of his task—a man need not necessarily be arrogant to consider himself capable of better than swatting flies—but he took this feeling in hand, reminding himself that he had chosen the discipline voluntarily, and so was in a poor position to resent whatever form it took; and seeing, also, that the very lowness and foolishness of the task must probably be by intention, as though testing from the start for the presence of any pride or individual assertiveness to be eradicated. No, he refused to be fooled so easily, refused to be fooled at all; he would stoop his pride to a proper use in the odd situation, if he were put into this cubical world to swat flies, why, he would pride himself upon swatting flies well.

Swatting—it now occurred to him that the conventional weapon for the purpose was not only absent; it had not even been mentioned. The common fly-swatter, a device so primitive it must have appeared at the dawn of history, so inexpensive that even the poorest families might own several, and so selectively efficient an instrument of the human will that not even insecticides could replace it—this instrument was not provided, and its absence gave Palen a moment of regret and even resentment; the fly-swatter he did not have seemed to him not only functional but beautiful as well, so that even the way of passively holding it in expectation would have had an emblematic quality as of the monarch's scepter, once perhaps a mace, and those elegant riding crops that officers used to carry long after their horses had vanished; it would have given an air.

If no fly-swatter, perhaps no fly? Perhaps, and the thought came to Palen as an instant of revelation, he had misinterpreted the problem altogether, and the instruction "to kill the flies in the room" had some allegorical, or even religious sense, as "to destroy the nasty black thoughts that feed on the filth of the self, and whose buzzing has but this one use, that it serves to keep the soul from sleeping in its foulness."

This resolution of the difficulty pleased him at first, but soon began to appear oversimplified. After all, he thought then, even if that is the meaning, it is only the first meaning, the one appearing on the surface; and surely one ought to

suspect the obvious and immediate in these matters. On re-
flection it seemed more likely that the instruction about killing the flies would be a riddle, such as any number of reli-
gions had availed themselves of for purposes of instruction,
of leading the mind outward from its fixities and falsehoods,
and the appropriate reply might be some kind of metaphor
—that the flies were thoughts was already a metaphor!—or
even an absurdity and a sheer irrelevance, a test of the mind's
ability to *leap* . . . where?

In an empty room, Palen now discovered, you cannot leap
very far. What was the opposite of a fly? the negation of a
fly? In an unfurnished room, even sheer irrelevance is hard
to come by, while absurdity, in the confines of a space so like
an absence, might well be impossible. But he was to *do* something, of that he felt certain.

Given so sparse a field to choose from, he decided on the
snowflakes, and there entered his mind at once a proverb
probably psychiatric in origin: he remembered having heard
that in some sense to count things was to kill them. So if you
equated, by way of axiom, snowflakes with flies, it followed
that counting the snowflakes was killing the flies; though
that bit of lore about counting summoned up in its wake
another, the memory that the Lord God of the Old Testa-
ment had set his face obstinately and definitely against num-
bering and the taking of a census, these newfangled notions
probably appearing to Him as unprofitably scientific or even
sociological, and somehow bound straight toward idolatry.
Still, Lord God, that particular bearded monster from childhood, need not be considered in the present situation. Palen
began to number the stars, thinking it best to begin at floor
level in a corner and work his way alternately up and down
and steadily clockwise around the room. In fact, he now saw,
the arithmetic learned in childhood would help him mightily, since the number for one wall would be identical with the

number for the opposite wall; while on account of the room's being a cube—one would have to check that also—the other walls might be done by the simple geometrical exercise of subtracting the number of snowflakes contained in the area of window and door.

At this moment he realized that he had no measuring instrument for doing all this, any more than he would have had a fly-swatter had real flies been in question. Palen sighed, feeling a trifle reduced. It would have been so simple, and the calculations themselves, easy as they were, would have afforded him a certain pleasure, not necessarily at his own ingenuity but at the marvelous thing the human intelligence was, with its ability to inherit the thoughts of men long dead. But he would have to count instead. He was thrown back, and probably this too was part of the purpose, upon the self as it was, alone and unaided by the devices of civilization. He was able to count, of course, that was true. But perhaps counting was not a device of civilization, perhaps it was something given? As the mathematicians were accustomed to say, God made the integers, man did all the rest.

Before beginning on the project, though, Palen allowed himself a few minutes of doubt, discouragement, irritable apathy, and cynicism concerning the whole course, however it might go, of what he had let himself in for—"the last expression," he hopefully put it to himself, "of the old, bad, unhappy civilian self." He permitted his memory to rove back over his former life, pausing upon common and familiar pleasures, trivial in themselves, certainly, but supremely important as embodying the one great pleasure of doing what you pleased. And now? Now this—this insensate activity that he was being compelled to do by his own free will: counting the wallpaper, wasn't that proverbially a sign of madness?

After a fit of this indulgence, Palen brought himself up short with the reminder that it had been the former life itself, with its pleasures that never pleased, its hunger-bearing fruits, the ill taste of its satisfactions, that had determined him to the present course. And here he was, ready to break down before the first and doubtless simplest exercise. That would be little faith indeed, for one who had so bravely or foolishly proposed so much, and whose object must be a happiness, even perhaps a power, transcending any possible image that the mind was able to form. So. If it began by counting, he would count.

What he had not counted on, however, was that the work might be not merely difficult, but positively a suffering to body and mind together. It went this way.

Palen knelt down in the corner (image, he remembered, of disgrace and contrition), and pointed to the first, lowest snowflake. Here was already a difficulty, for owing to the nature of wallpaper it happened that some of the flakes on the wall to his left overlapped onto the wall to his right, where he wanted to begin. Well, that was easy enough, he would leave them out, take them last, after making the whole circuit. Only he had to remember that he had taken this decision and not the alternative one to count them at first; it was one more thing to remember, and even on account of its simplicity seemed disproportionately a burden. Still, it was decided, and he started counting. But the damnable naturalism of the makers of the wallpaper was such that their snowflakes didn't fall in straight lines, *more geometrico*, but in a helter and a dance; it was distracting, too, that the same impulse to naturalism had made the designer provide several different shapes for his snowflakes, to suggest to the mind the well-known scientific fact that no two snowflakes were alike. Getting used to this circumstance alone made it necessary for Palen to start over several times. But he found in his favor that it was possible, by holding one hand for a boundary marker, so to limit the space under consideration that the small starry shapes formed momentary patterns that could successfully be counted, and if, with patience, he could hold out till he reached a seam—though he dared not look up, he figured that the seam must be not more than a yard away—there would be plain sailing from then on, a matter merely of multiplication. Still, he could have wept for the want of a pencil; how well things would go with a pencil, you would circle the flakes, or even number them, or check them off as you went. . . . The thought made him lose count, and he had to start over.

The practice, however, was definitely bringing about an improvement in his ability, though at the same time fatigue was perceptibly beginning to appear as a factor; something, he observed, that entered his awareness in the form of denial as he said to himself with surprise, "I'm not at all tired yet," and realized it was the cramp in his knees, the ache in his back, the forming of tears in his eyes, that said this. Rising from his knees he stooped, he stood bent over, gradually straightened up, tilted his head back, raised his arm with pointing, counting finger, stood on tiptoe, counting all the while aloud, while the numbers grew monstrous. . . . Because of the cube shape of the room he could not reach anywhere near the ceiling, and up there the stars blinked and occulted before his dazed eyes, his wavering finger, the dizziness of the mind.

And the numbers grew so rapidly, they too were a physical burden to be borne out on the sighing tide of the breath and only to become fully articulate on the last digit. It had seemed so simple at first! Only ten integers to remember, plus one more, the changing first one after every ten; but then, at a hundred, it was two more; and at a thousand three; and when he reached ten thousand. . . .

He did not reach ten thousand, or anything like it. A little flicker of motion at the corner of his eye, of real motion in the midst of that dancing stasis, compelled him to turn his head even as he realized that in doing so he had already lost count and would have to begin again. Looking up and back at the window he saw that while he was engaged in his ordeal the sky had clouded over, and snow had just now begun to fall, a few flakes that even as he stared seemed to increase in number.

Palen sat down—it was not quite that, rather he fell in a sitting position—and put his head in his hands. He shut his eyes, and then rubbed them hard with his knuckles, so that he saw against a burning background a dance of black sparks that even his tears could not quench. These tears were not quite childish tears of outrage and frustration, but neither were they quite the tears of fatigue and strained attention; rather they shared the sponsorship of both, and to Palen this seemed just, correct, and dignified: something that went together in a world where other things did not appear to possess this property.

Thus he sat for some time, though in his changed state of mind the casual "some time" seemed inappropriate though he used it himself. It was more like being in eternity "for some time." It was not only his having been deprived of his watch; he would not in any event have consulted his watch. Alone in the empty room, it came to him to think, "It doesn't count," and "nothing counts." The last especially, perhaps owing to the insoluble ambiguity in the means provided by language for saying it, whatever it was, made an immense, a near absolute, appeal to his feelings; it was at once a mystery and a consolation in the presence of that mystery.

Very gradually, however, Palen came to himself, his thoughts began to sort themselves out in something like reasonable order, and he began in spite of himself to wrestle again with his strange situation. He remembered, to begin with, that the insane business of counting the snowflakes on the wallpaper had been entirely his own invention; nothing in the initial situation as given made him do this, he did it on his own. That was an appalling thought, but yet had a dignity to it if you compared it with the nonsense of numbers he had just put himself through. He had made a mistake, admitted. But even the existence of a mistake proved the existence of a correct solution, or at any rate suggested the likelihood of one.

"All right, I made a mistake, I was wrong. But I am able to acknowledge it." And the thing to do when you perceived that you had made a mistake, as Palen knew even from school days, was to go back along the chain of reasoning—the thread of reasoning, more likely, in this instance—and see just where you made the first step off the true path.

When he attempted to apply this principle, Palen was upset, and even a little frightened, at the spectacle of his own glibness—or the glibness of a mind that moved, it seemed, independently of his will—at getting from here to there. It was even very difficult, at first, to remember what he had started from only a short while ago, the instruction to kill the flies in the room, the relation of that to fly-swatters, the negation of both terms, the translation of that negation into other terms symmetrical with the first . . . leading to the madly irrelevant decision that counting snowflakes on the wall was "the same thing as" killing flies.

Palen believed he had learned something from this sudden and terrible experience—now he looked back upon it he saw how ridiculous and stupid it was, but reminded himself all the same that it had indeed been sudden and terrible. He thought he understood now why the first instruction of the master to the disciple in any mystery had to be a deep and thoroughgoing distrust of the reason—just because it "reasoned" so very well.

The reason's work was so exclusively concerned with single threads isolated from the pattern that finally it took the thread it followed for the whole design. Whereas—

And now he saw. Pattern! Design! how foolish to believe

that wallpaper ever came otherwise! He had been pursuing the foolish futility of a savage, or of those half-sophisticated persons who believe that scientific truth emerges of itself out of the collection of large numbers of facts.

The wallpaper—supposing, as he helplessly had to, the wallpaper to be somehow relevant—had a pattern. And perhaps part of his task here (while waiting for those improbable or nonexistent flies) was to elucidate the pattern. Upon this consideration he forced himself to open his eyes, and keep them open although the sight of those dark blue snowflakes made him sleepy almost at once.

Palen advised himself that there was no hurry, not this time. One must just sit and contemplate—sit and stare, would be the better, because the stupider, expression. Under no circumstances was the active intelligence to intervene with its plausible suggestions. After all, it was a point of faith that the assigned task might be very difficult, but not in the nature of things impossible. One must simply sit still. Indeed, that might be precisely the mystical import of an instruction to kill the flies in a room where no flies were: that is, do nothing—the chief recommendation of the great religious of every persuasion from the beginning of the world.

But where—this problem proposed itself inevitably and at once—where did simply looking divide itself from looking and thinking at once? Palen found it impossible not to observe right at the start, for instance, that the seam he had counted on reaching did not exist; the wallpaper went in one unbroken reach from wall to wall and floor to ceiling. Did it possibly go all around the room in a similar manner? He was about to go over to a corner and inspect this more closely, but reminded himself of his very recent decision to sit still: here he was, about to break it almost at once.

And then, this pattern that he intuited, or believed in, or postulated—would it be large or small? How large? How small? At the extreme limits, any two flakes might form a pattern duplicated in any two other flakes; or there might be no repetition whatever over the whole wall, though if that were so one might test the hypothesis that one wall duplicated its opposite, as though it were a mirror.

The mad thought that one of the walls might *be* a mirror hit Palen so suddenly that he shut his eyes tight once again, and kept them that way until reason came to offer the soothing suggestion that Palen too would have to be reflected in such a wall, since he . . . and so on and so on, after the manner of reason.

"—If I exist," said Palen aloud and with an unnecessarily assertive laugh. But he allowed himself to be persuaded all the same into opening his eyes and being reassured, if that was the word, that either he did not exist or one wall was not a mirror; though as to the question of symmetry between one and another wall, that would take patient study which he did not feel quite up to at this time.

Again he was looking, only looking. But from nowhere, and at terrible speed—you could not not have thought it, once you had thought it—there formed in his mind the hypothesis that, on the wallpaper as in nature, there were no two snowflakes alike. At least, Palen could not remember having seen any two alike.

Once opened up, the possible field of this thought appeared to extend indefinitely. Palen had always unthinkingly accepted it as a scientific fact that no two snowflakes were alike; their differences-in-sameness, the elaboration of infinite variations upon the one unpromising hexagonal construction, were always being held up as witness to the unfailing delicacy and artistry, as well as deathly fecundity, of Nature. But now that he thought of this bit of lore, the difficulty or impossibility of ever demonstrating any such thing became for Palen the most obvious and glaring fact in the entire situation; and the well-known scientific fact a piece of preposterous scientific arrogance on the one hand and of gossipy superstition on the other; yet he would have said that he had "always thought" it. Why, even the difficulty of keeping a snowflake unmelted long enough to make possible the gathering of all other snowflakes for purposes of comparison—even the making of an inclusive catalogue—and even that would not account for the snowflakes that had fallen in past winters and were irretrievably gone, the snowflakes of yesteryear—and even this and even that, until Palen realized that he was doing something suspiciously close to counting again, and, with an effort, stopped.

Simultaneously with the conclusion of this meditation he directed his attention outward and realized two things. The snow outside the window had ceased from falling. And somewhere in the room a fly that had been buzzing probably for some time, was buzzing.

Digressions Around a Crow

ONE AFTERNOON IN midsummer my son David appeared on the scene followed by a crow. Improbable spectacle, but there it was; the crow not flying, but walking at a distance of some six feet behind the child. A recent shower had left large puddles on the lane, and David walked through the puddles, while the crow detoured around them. My wife watched, I watched, as the two of them in line astern proceeded across the lawn. Suzy the dog and Alfred the cat also watched, somewhat alertly.

"This is my crow," David announced, with a prepared indifference. "He follows me everywhere." My wife Peggy, who responds to even the happiest emergencies with food, had already said, "He must be hungry, poor thing," and gone into the house.

"What is so special about you?" I said to my son, "that a crow should follow you?" I was chagrined. Given my long-standing sympathy with bird life of all domestically available sorts, it seemed to me as though a bird interested in forming human acquaintances might reasonably have come to me first.

"He just likes me, I guess," said David.

The crow was now walking and hopping tentatively about, investigating the gravel of the drive. He picked up a pebble, swallowed it, then coughed it up; he did this a number of times. Presently my wife appeared with a pan of bread moistened in water.

"Watch out for Suzy and Alfred," she said.

"He doesn't mind," said David of the crow, and this seemed to be true. Moreover, both cat and dog were, for the moment at least, more surprised than overtly hostile; and neither of them, probably, was able to move fast enough to catch a full grown crow in command of his faculties. Still, I thought already that the crow's attitude to these animals was extremely casual.

"I'll feed him," David said to Peggy. "He won't trust you." Indeed, the crow, almost insolently familiar with a small human being, appeared to have reservations about large ones, and would give a nervous compound hop-and-flutter backwards at our near approach, without, however, flying away.

When David sat down with the pan of wet bread, there was at first the other difficulty; the crow wasn't timid, but David was. A close view of that black, metallic beak made him tend at the last instant to throw the bread rather than give it; but this was soon overcome, and the crow was swallowing the bread, some of it permanently, along with some stones which David once in a while included in his diet. This may have been a bit thoughtless of the boy, but after all, I thought, whose crow is it? and I refrained from making speeches. Anyhow, the bird did not appear to distinguish in any absolute manner bread from stone. Sometimes he would take a piece of bread and put it carefully under a stone for future reference—he didn't generally forget these things, by the way, but was able to find them again—while sometimes he would take a stone and put that under a stone.

"His name is Joe," said David. "Joe Crow. Here, Joey, Joey."

The crow was silent, but continued to let himself be fed, and even stroked.

"He looks so bedraggled," Peggy said. "Look, the feathers on his head are almost grey. He must be starved."

"Probably yearling plumage," I said, not above introducing an authoritative note of fraudulent lore into the discussion.

"Now we have a cat and a dog and a crow," said David happily.

And so it seemed we did, for the crow began reporting daily to our house, first to be fed and then to play—with David and with the other children who turned up. It was an enchanted time, and gave us a kind of mythological status in the neighborhood. That black shape, with his black shadow, became an eerie, comic presence, walking behind the child, flying above him, perching deep in the green jungle overhead.

II

By the second day, Joey had moved on from moistened bread to pieces of salami; in keeping, said I, with the first law of the feeding of animals, that it always moves in the direction of greater expense. A grudging, unlovely remark, but I was remembering the grosbeaks who came to the feeder every winter. They would sit there, high up out of Alfred's reach, a dozen at least of them, with others resting on the clothesline when they weren't fighting for a place at the trough, and chomp away at sunflower seeds (not inexpensive) until they could barely fly. Nor did their serious gluttony prevent them from meanwhile braying and squawking and squabbling, so that they looked like a collection of Dodger fans eating peanuts in the old days at Ebbetts Field. Unlike the relatively polite nuthatch or even bluejay, these birds did not take seeds away by ones to devour in silence, but sat there crunching and munching and dropping the shells on the porch along with their other droppings. When nothing was left but shells, they would bicker digestively for a while, then lurch heavily away through the air; but as soon as I replenished the supply they seemed to know it, or they had told their friends in the interim, and a large collection of grosbeaks again appeared.

It is part of the ethics of feeding birds in winter that you cannot leave off without feeling some twinges in the conscience, as though the beaked and taloned harpies of a small remorse were at you. So these grosbeaks had cost me a very fair sum, and my remark may be taken as directed at them, and not at Joey.

Besides, in return for the charm of his company, we were so obviously doing him good! In a few days, on a diet of salami,

the ashen complexion of the feathers of his head deepened to
its proper blue-black and rainbow shine; a few days more,
and his voice began to be heard: the standard crow noise,
written by humans 'caw'—and yet extremely expressive, so
that if you couldn't say just yet what it was expressive of, you
nevertheless found yourself thinking that a few days more
might make all the difference: either Joey would articulate
more clearly, or you would understand better, and he would
be saying something like, "In actual fact, the last place I was
at they didn't feed me this good."

Or something. For if the first thing one does with a wild
creature come to the door is feed it—unless it is so obviously
large and threatening (lion) or otherwise noxious (skunk,
king cobra) as to make this inadvisable—still, the second thing
one does is form a theory or two to account for its presence.

"He must have been brought up by human beings from a
fledgling," I said. "Wild birds just do not come and make up
to human beings in this manner on their own."

"Probably the owners moved away," said Peggy, "and left
the poor thing to starve."

Peggy's view of human behavior would make such an
action about par, but I favored a less vicious image, of a
kindly, white-haired old lady; she was doing the cleaning, the
screen door stood open for the better beating of carpets and
shaking-out of mops and rags; the clever bird (crows notor-
iously are) managed to open its cage and escape to a freedom
it was no longer equipped to endure.

"He is a crow anthropologist," said David, "and the crows
have sent him to investigate people."

"Is that what they teach you in that Social Studies book?" I
asked. But this theory seemed, finally, about as good as the
others. For you have theories because you are a human being,
and that is what human beings do; not because the theories
are likely to account for the sudden presence of a pet crow.

Or rather, as I was at pains to emphasize to David, not a pet but a visiting crow.

"He doesn't belong to us," I said on several occasions in my disagreeably pedantic way. "He is a free agent, and as long as he wants to come to us that's fine, but I don't want you bringing him into the house or putting him in a cage, or anything like that. Things are exactly and beautifully right just as they are."

"He can't go back to the flock," said David. "They'll kill him for being with humans." To this remark, with its combination of scientific-sounding ornithology and animistic magic, I was unable to say anything except that it contradicted the crow-anthropologist theory. All the same, Joey evidently did go somewhere at night, and I rather thought it must be back among his wild fellows, who could be heard cawing mightily for an hour before dusk in the woods below the house; the wonder was that he came back.

Not that he came back exclusively to us. Several times David reported dejectedly having seen Joey breakfasting at the Durands', or hanging around Robert's lawn at lunch time.

"Well, that's the good thing about it," said I, "that he doesn't *belong* to anybody." All the same, I was ready to be a little peeved myself. There is a sneaky distinction to being selected friend and patron by a wild creature, and one tended to resent, for Joey, his making himself common.

Still, it turned out that he was with us more than with others; maybe our salami was better. Our expectation got to the point at which Peggy said we would have to do something about him in the winter; a box, maybe, on the porch, where he could shelter from the worst of the weather.

III *Digression on Birds*

For us amateurs—what Grandma, God bless her, might have called nature-noshers—a relation of this kind with a wild creature has a marvelous charm; as though a beautiful, inaccessible world comes close and begins to open itself; an idea of edenic innocence and trust looks wildly possible, one dreams of speaking the language of birds, of understanding. . . . O Tarzan, Mowgli, Bomba, Siegfried (to grow up a bit).

My own adventures among the birds had been few and accidental; two anecdotes will sum up the range.

Once I came on a starling standing on a path. He didn't move at my approach, and soon I saw he was not so much standing as propped up stiffly on his feet and tail, like a three-legged stool. He hardly twitched as I picked him up and bore him tenderly home. Probably he had cracked his head on a branch (birds are sometimes not so bright at flying as we suppose) and was now in a catalepsy deep as Socrates'; still, I felt as proud and cherishing as could be, and hoped someone would be around to see me. All the upshot of it was, however, that I stood the starling in a safe place, sprinkled drops of water on his head as one might do with a fighter between rounds—he blinked a bit, and stood quite still, and half an hour later, when I was no longer paying him much attention, he took off, so that was that.

Then there was the yearling gull I picked up on the beach, since he too seemed unable to get out of the way as I came along. I kept him in a liquor carton for a couple of days, and tried to tempt him with cat food and even canned herring, but it was a pretty sick bird I had foolishly made myself responsible for—from his green, liquid, and foul-smelling excretions even I could understand that—and finally I had an inspiration: I would take the poor thing down to the Bird Sanctuary in the salt marshes a dozen miles away. *They* would know what to do.

I can't say, really, whether this plan succeeded or failed. My arrival with the sick gull in his carton coincided with the gathering of a group of binoculared bird-watchers who were about to be shown around the premises by a guide, and this guide, not without a touch of impatience at being interrupted, took one look at the bird and said:

"Botulism."

"I thought," said I, "you might know what to do for the poor thing."

"Oh, yes," he replied, briskly confident; and all those bird-watchers gathered round him with admiration amounting to reverence written on their faces. "Hundreds of 'em die of it every year on this coast—it's the garbage they eat. Best turn you can do him is wring his neck."

"!?" (indignation, horror).

"If you're squeamish about it, what you do is, you put him under the rear wheel and back over him."

I could see that this was a touch strong even for the bird-watchers, though if anything it probably increased their admiration they were feeling for Their Leader as a man who knew how tough things really were in this vale of tears—they would get a fine sense of inexpensive stoicism out of it. Whereas I—

"Oh dear," I said, "I don't know if I could do that."

"If you don't," said the guide, "he'll die anyhow."

And I didn't, and he did.

A painful business, though I can't see how it was my fault.

Professionals, anyhow, must necessarily be more austere about Nature, and less full of fine feelings. After all, they will point out, if Nature provided no checks, such as cats, on the robin population (for instance), in a few years the world would be so full of robins we should each of us be standing on a couple. Not an agreeable image.

My friend Thomas is a professional, member of the Society, bird-bander, trapper, writer on ornithological subjects, whom I have sometimes consulted on questions in this area. Once, when I reported to him on the phone what would have been a rarity if it happened to be what I thought it was, he ran through a list of characteristics which might reduce my find to something a good deal less spectacular, and then seemed sufficiently convinced to say:

"In this instance, I think you'd be justified in collecting a specimen."

"What?"

"Oh, yes. The Society wouldn't accept any report on this kind of thing except at the end of a gun; you'll have to have the skin."

A rather casual attitude, I thought, toward mortality; and a great price for a poor bird to pay, only for being a thousand miles out of place. In fairness to Thomas, though, I must allow his attitude toward humanity to include a similar factor of objectivity: the reduction of the race by, say, one half, seems to him a reasonable remedy for most of our troubles. As he has pointed out, if you have two major problems— overpopulation and nuclear weapons—one of them will sooner or later be viewed, not without reason, as the solution to the other.

IV *Digression on Dogs*

Practically everyone living in the countryside keeps a dog, if not more than one. I don't know what it is, there must be a myth about dogs and people. All behavior, anyhow, is a parody of behavior, so it is plain that the thoughtless automatism with which people in rural areas procure dogs for themselves or their kids must reflect some deep, unexamined presumption about How Things Are, or How They Used To Be.

These dogs are often extremely fierce, or at any rate they produce that impression. You cannot, in my part of the country, go for a walk of over two hundred feet without being barked at, growled at, sniffed up and down, and capered before. I carry a heavy stick whenever I go out. And yet I can scarcely complain, since as you have observed I too keep a dog. Suzy began life as a purebred beagle, but in the process of growth all the purity began moving to the rear, until now only her tail is purebred beagle: a very nice dog.

All the same, I do complain. And I introduce this question of dogs because of my worry about them on Joey's account. I admired our crow's calm and even gay insouciance with reference to dogs, but I could not commend his prudence. Not only would he provoke the neighboring dogs by flying along beside them as they ran, or just above their necks, and often in such a relation with the sun that they appeared to be foolishly pursuing his shadow;—not only would he dive on them and swoop past between their ears in a most unexpected and probably unsettling way, whereat even Suzy's ruff began to bristle;—but he would also, as a matter of course, walk around right behind one of them, often at a distance of no more than a foot.

The dogs chiefly concerned were, apart from Suzy, the following: Ranger, Ginger, Klaus, and Clancy.

If the perfection of a species is its beauty, Klaus was a beautiful dachshund.

Ranger and Ginger, either of whom might without injustice have been called Scrounger, went from house to house at feeding time.

Clancy had only three legs. This was the result of surgery which saved his life after he had been, doubtless through his own fault, hit by a car.

Human attitudes to Clancy reflected perhaps something of our attitudes to deformity and the deformed among ourselves, in three stages, thus: first, a deep horror, causing people to avert their eyes; second, a generous sympathy, from the perception that this brave creature got on very well on his three legs; third, the disillusioned certainty that Clancy used his deformity as a reproach and a weapon of advantage, to produce in human beings exactly the shamed embarrassment and remorse produced by the legless veteran selling pencils on the windiest corner. Altogether, about as attractive as Richard the Third.

I made as clear as I could to this crew of wretched opportunists (including Suzy) that I regarded Joe the Crow as being under my special protection; and was successful in getting from each of them a look of understanding though not of sympathy—for it is probable that our view of dogs as "nearly human," our exaggerated opinion of their intelligence, are based only on this, that by long association with ourselves dogs have developed an extreme sensitivity to guilt; conscience and remorse form the whole range to which the antennae of their supposed intelligence are tuned.

Probably all I accomplished in this way was to exacerbate in these dogs a mortal sensitivity to Joey, a sensitivity whose comparable progression in human beings may be seen to run from irritated curiosity to furtive lust to anxiety to desperate actions.

v *Digression on People*

Having a crow for family totem made us to a certain extent the envy of the neighborhood, but this view was not unanimous. It began to be said by a few that the crow terrorized very small children. All I could say to this was that they must be very silly children indeed, if they imagined that pleasant-tempered and altogether friendly and upright crow was going to do them any harm.

Then an embattled mother came to report that Joey had seized and flown away with her daughter's rattle—a silver rattle by way of being an heirloom, with (she said) the marks of her own and her mother's first teeth in it.

"Too bad," I said, "Obviously irreplaceable, isn't it?"

"Obviously," said she.

"He's not *our* crow," I said, "he only visits."

There followed some dark threats about what husbands, hers and others, had said about shooting the crow if it bothered the children. You might have thought this great *Lammergeier* of a crow was going to pick some kid up by its diaper and take off over the mountains. I assured the woman this could not happen, and even offered to show her an encyclopedia article which should put her mind at rest concerning the possible payload of any given bird relative to its own weight; but she left unappeased.

My neighbor Mr Holsapple, a writer on philosophical subjects for ladies' magazines, also made a difficulty. A portly bearded man, Mr Holsapple appeared one morning at breakfast, accepted a cup of coffee, and said:

"I am, to the best of my knowledge, a humane and tolerant person, without more than the normal amount of aggression—"

"Have you done something wrong?" Peggy asked.

"I am aware," he went on, "that this world has every title to be called a jungle, and that nature red in tooth and claw is everywhere around us."

"That is one view," I said, "but at the same time you must allow that recent researches have cut down very considerably on that sort of naive Darwinism—the work of Ashley Montagu, for example, would tend to stress rather the benign and even loving elements in—"

"You may say so," replied Mr Holsapple. "You may say so. You may tell me that the man-eating shark, for instance, is largely a myth, contradicted by all the really verifiable evidence; that barracuda and pirana do not really eat human flesh, that even lion and tiger will not attack humans except when driven by extreme hunger. Still, it remains that the carnivores both large and small must eat death daily in order to exist—yourself for instance." He pointed to a leftover piece of bacon on my plate.

In the discussion following, it turned out that Mr Holsapple was herbivorous, and had been for many years.

"Since the day," he told us, "that, doing the shopping for

my wife, I walked into the supermarket and took one good look at a lamb chop, and realized all at once what it was—a piece of a beast like myself. I saw through the cellophane, I'll tell you that."

A further discussion dealt with man's place in nature, the idea of health, and possible scientific or totemic relations between meat-eating and hostility.

"So this morning," Mr Holsapple said, "as I sat down to my work table, which I keep before the picture window giving on my lawn—as I was composing myself to get on with this piece I am writing, a piece about Education For The Future, I was really quite disturbed to see that crow of yours—"

"He's not our crow," I said, "he only visits us."

"—that crow of yours alight on the grass before my eyes, and there proceed to dismember and devour a small mouse."

Mr Holsapple was being to a certain extent humorous, of course. But it turned out that he was being to a certain extent serious as well.

"I wish you would tell that crow of yours," was the way he put it, "not to bring dead animals—or living ones—to my lawn and devour them in my sight. I find that sort of thing physically unsettling, as well as wrong in principle."

"I'm sorry," said I, "but I don't really see what I can do about your trouble, Mr Holsapple. The crow is, after all, a friend, rather than a pet in any ordinary sense."

"Would you let your friends eat mice on a neighbor's lawn?"

"Just a minute!" said Peggy. "How do you know this was our crow?"

"Well," Mr Holsapple began, "I simply saw this large black bird, and I assumed—"

"I suppose," Peggy pursued, "you would be able to identify this bird by some particular markings, or characteristic individual look?"

"It seemed a reasonable presumption," Mr Holsapple said, "that this crow was your crow."

"How many crows would you estimate lived in this neighborhood?"

"All the same," Mr Holsapple said, as he got up, "I do wish you could convince that crow not to eat things on my lawn, at least not in the mornings.

"I've never wanted to make trouble," he added as he went out the door.

Poor Mr Holsapple! Ah, Peggy! Ah, Portia!

VI

So, for a long and rather enchanted spell, Joey came every day, to be fed and then to play. The children, except the littlest, came, and when they ran down the lane Joey would rise and dive past them, tickling their necks with his wing, or with the black shadow of his wing. Joey would get tired faster than the children, though, and then he would sit in a tree, or on the roof, till he caught his breath and felt ready to play some more.

Sometimes in the morning or evening, after feeding, he would walk importantly around the car, inspecting his reflexion in the metal of the bumpers where they curved under. This was certainly a stage of development higher than that of dog or cat, who view a mirror as a strictly neutral and non-representational surface. What Joey saw, though, was not himself but another crow, whom he pecked at with a rather musical clang.

Now summer drew toward its close, there was a dusty silver to the still green wall of the woods, the heat began to have an indefinable feel of embers, and baseball was one day suddenly abandoned for football; which I mention only because Joey found this game more confusing than baseball, where it was easy for him to follow the runners around; and on the first day, he was hit in air by a pass. It knocked the wind out of him, he sat down suddenly in the grass, and stayed for a few minutes, but for the rest was neither damaged nor dismayed.

When school began, Joey followed David down to the village—human pride can rarely have had an occasion for soaring higher than this—and produced an educational crisis by perching outside various classrooms successively and peering in at the children in such a way as to prevent, it was said, work. On several occasions, David was told off to walk the crow back up the hill; whereon Peggy would have to drive him back to school to elude Joey.

We had by now even begun planning the crow some winter quarters on the porch, and agreeing that, in view of the severity of the winter weather, he might have to be, on some occasions, let in the house—though only if he freely decided to enter.

And then, of course, he went away, or he stayed away, or however you would put it. Suddenly—it could not have been otherwise than suddenly—he wasn't there any more. Had he gone South? Some crows did, and others didn't; there were always a few around in the winter.

David found a few black feathers in the path, over near where Clancy lived.

We did not condemn Clancy on this thin evidence. I looked at him, and he looked at me. But I looked at all the dogs, and decided their mute and universal aspect of guilt covered, concealed, and overwent the commission of any particular crime.

So that, I guess, is the mournful point, that nature returned to nature; that the wilderness, which had seemed about to speak, suddenly changed its—mind? or whatever you would call it. We were again isolated, with our dogs, in humanity, and the boundary which had been near to being dissolved at one little place was drawn again with a great firmness.

Was this the ordained result of our longing tenderness toward wild things? It looked to be so. If only, we think, if only they would come to us, they would learn how kindly we are, we humans, how generous, how loving. And here one of them had, one miserable crow, and almost without doubt died of the experiment.

Just as our dog, Suzy, at the seashore, chases wildly after the sanderlings, and when they fly looks mournful, as though to say: "I only wanted to play with them." But the sanderlings probably know better than she the extent of her wants, for she would have eaten them if she could; so with ourselves, who humanize wild nature in our thoughts, and in the reality are able only to destroy, though we do so—this is the worst of it—out of love and yearning.

There is one thought minimally happier than that, though. As between a death and a disappearance the evidence was imperfect, and not absolutely conclusive. Joey might have gone away, to return in the spring. Or some other bird-brained notion might have taken him, just to abandon us; maybe he was bored.

Anyhow, for better or worse, as my wife had suggested to Mr Holsapple, we do not readily recognize the individuals of a wild species; bird-watching only rarely takes us that far, and we do not make those keen, subtle, unconscious discriminations of eye, ear, hair, pimple and chin which identify our human acquaintances. So, now it is spring, whenever a crow or two goes by we call out after it, "Joey," and again, "Joey," thus far without other result than a generic and rather cheerful "caw." But there seems some hapless charm in the unspoken belief that, somewhere among the anonymous many, a single crow with a name is thinking, even rather bad thoughts, about us.

Three thousand copies of this first edition have been set in Monotype
Bembo and printed by The Stinehour Press. The paper is Mohawk
Superfine. The book was bound by Robert Burlen & Son.

The title page and the dust jacket were
designed by John Benson.